JUST ALEX

Jessica Badrick

Order this book online at www.trafford.com
or email orders@trafford.com

Most Trafford titles are also available at major online book retailers.

Printed in the United States of America.

ISBN: 978-1-4669-4219-6 (sc)
ISBN: 978-1-4669-4218-9 (e)

Trafford rev. 06/18/2012

 www.trafford.com

North America & international
toll-free: 1 888 232 4444 (USA & Canada)
phone: 250 383 6864 ♦ fax: 812 355 4082

*"I chose my kids, I chose my family, I chose my love . . .
but I think I made the wrong choice. I don't think I can do this . . ."*

CHAPTER 1

CHOICE MADE

"Do I even want to know how this happened" Dr. Wittson sighed shining a flash light in my eyes trying to get them to follow the light for the third time.

I was less dizzy and had been cleaned up some but I could still only smell blood. I watched him put a bandage over my stitches. It was the first cut I had since I stopped. I had been really careful not to get cuts; I had scraps, scratches, road burn, plenty of bruises but never any cuts. "A broken plastic spoon, one of the girls" The stoic answer had nothing to do with my throbbing head and everything to do with the look on every ones face. Once you're a cutter ever one assumes you're going to do it again and that every little injury is from you no matter how bad it hurt or anything else.

"Don't give me that I asked what happened."

I sighed "They got into a fight, I did my job she swung my arm was there. I am fine now that the flash backs have stopped."

"Hmm, well, you're going home you have a concussion but I bet you knew that. And your not to smack you head on any more floors, your mother is not someone I wish on my bad side and Dave doesn't either. Also call your Aunt Kate.

"I can't I have a preschool meeting for Paul in twenty minute."

"Then go home and call your aunt."

"Fine" I rolled my eyes, I had no intention of calling anyone, but I wanted out of the infirmary.

I ran and checked on the girls showing them I was ok no serious damage; I thanked Greg for filling out the paper work, and then hugged Anthony good night. I made the thirty minute drive in fifteen thankful I was not pulled over or worse.

Uncle Donavan looked at my arm "Klutz he muttered.

"Psycho teenager actually; how late am I?"

"Thirty nanoseconds, they just went in, to see if you were already here."

"Grazie (thanks)" I rushed into the school after my uncle Christian and caught up no problem.

"Oh there you are" He shoved and inhaler at me "Ana called, are you alright?"

"Yeah, Crazy teenager, I am fine, more than relieved I had brought a change of clothes and that the double vision stopped before I had to drive."

"Mmm I don't condone driving with a concussion and I here you made quite a mess."

I blushed "Sorry."

*   *   *

We got to the Preschool wing and had to wait I sat watching all the little preschoolers; they looked so cute in their uniforms. Mom had said the year I was born they made it mandatory that all schools have uniforms, but it was still a place of honor to wear the sleek black and sharp red of Crimson Academy. Paul played with blocks as we waited; I worked on getting my head not to throb. We waited a good half hour. By then there were only two children left in the waiting room, besides Paul and they were climbing a book case.

"JEFFERY! CLAUDIA!" The lady sounded on her last straw "GET DOWN, NOW! Sorry" She addressed us "Some days my grandchildren forget they are not animals; Jeffery is five and Claudia is four" She smiled. "I am Mrs. Livingston and you" She spoke to Paul must be Paul."

"Does I gets to wear a ooniform too? I have one for Saturdays it's called a G and next year Mr. Ear Ic says I can pactice ka atee like *MY Antony*."

"We will see" She smiled at him. To me she said "He is very friendly and outgoing."

"Thank-you" I stood shaking her hand "I am Alex Williams and this is my uncle, Christian. Ana is working today and is unable to make it."

"I went over the paper work you mailed in"

"Ana" I smiled "She has better memory and hand writing." I was nervous and rambling.

"Ok" She smiled "Ana. Anyway, I remember both of your mothers and your uncles. I use to teach Shakespeare in the high school. Your mother was . . ."

"Witch one ma'am?"

"Jess" Uncle Christian laughed "Sorry but only Mio Piccolo can cause that face in a person."

"Well, yes she was extremely smart, though. Nalanie was a pleasure also; I was sorry to hear of her passing. But your mother . . . let's just say she left an impacting impression." Mrs. Livingston forced a smile. It was nice to have someone recognize Mama for something other than music or gay pride events, although it sounded bad like when all the fourth grade teachers thought Nick would be just like Christopher and Christian just because we are brothers.

Uncle Christian stifled a laugh and muttered boots.

"Anyway, Paul and I are going to go talk and play to determine how much speech attention he needs, while you fill out these."

I sat and read the sheets. It was about allergies, medicine and special needs Paul didn't have any of that but under things the teacher should

3

know I wrote adopted, brother in C.H.T.D.C. Bilingual: English/ Italian. Then I paced trying to shake the head ache, Uncle Christian felt I should have been sitting he was probably right as I was getting dizzy but I didn't want to tell him if I sat still I would be giving into the oh so tempting desire to go back to cutting and I refused. I loved being a dad way too much, and my job and my life where I am not completely numb with friends and family in it.

"Ok Paul we will see you soon. Can you please sit with your uncle, while I speak to your father?"

"Ok Ma'am" He smiled and bounced over to Uncle Christian.

I let out a breath I hadn't realized I had been holding when I heard Paul had remembered to use his best manners, as I followed her in to her office."

"Well he is very smart advanced even, in most areas but defiantly has some speech delay he will grow out of it but he will be a great model student for our spring program starting February twenty-third."

"Thank you Ma'am"

"You're welcome" She hand me the rest of the registration paper work. "So you know Crimson . . ."

"I know ma'am, I graduated from Crimson class of 2024."

"Ok then we will see you January twenty eighth for orientation and uniform ordering."

"Thank-you so much" We shook hands again.

*   *   *

I looked at the clock it was one thirty am but I could not sleep. All I could think about was the cut on my arm and how bad I wanted to make one next to it. I began to cry I had worked so hard to clean up, and it had been so long I didn't want to go through it all again. I refused to relapse I was stronger than that. I had just started to feel like I fit in somewhere. I began to panic and went down stairs and balled up on the couch shaking and crying, shortly after there was a hand on my ankle and one my back.

"I am sorry I woke you" I sobbed harder, already knowing it was my mothers.

Mama lifted my bandaged arm "This, this will pass."

"I'm so . . ."

"We were not asleep sweetie" Mom patted my leg.

Mama pulled me in to her arms "Ooff, this has been a while" She laughed "You have gotten rather heavy."

"I can't stop crying and I am panicking and I don't know why" I sobbed in to her shoulder.

"Then just cry" Mama said "I cried for a long time after I stopped your body is just readjusting to having to cope with your emotions."

"I . . . I . . ." My words fail and I shifted a little I needed mom too.

Without my telling her she knew and I was wrapped safe between my mothers' arms "You are never too old to be so emotionally exhausted that you need your mommy or to cry."

They held me tight like when I was little and I cried myself to sleep, it had be a very long time since I had done that.

CHAPTER 2

REACHING OUT IS NOT EASY JUST NECESSARY

Mama had told me many times about when she stopped cutting in fact other than her music it was the only thing she herself willingly shared about her past with me. And she told me many people cry and fall apart and that it could just be the concussion messing with me. I knew they had worried when I hadn't fallen apart like Mama had, not that they wanted me too; but I guess parts of my actions were a bit suspicious. And if I had a repeat of last night now Dave was going to lock me up for zombie impersonations.

"Uhg" I groaned looking in the bathroom mirror trying for the fourth time to wash the bright red tear stains off my face. I was pissed with myself I had not done this four years ago and had spent three years since telling teens it was ok and normal. Dave had put me on filing; he felt I need a day away from being beat on by wild kids. I think he had looked at me and was worried I was sick again. I was still crying on and off and it was infuriating to try and wash the stains off only to start crying again. It made me feel weak that stupid minor insignificant things could make me cry. If Dave had noticed he was not saying anything and for that I was thankful.

"They don't wash off" Greg came in "They only look that bright to you, to everyone else you just look tired, but they won't wash off."

I looked at him in shock.

"You aren't the only one to ever cry Al, I cried for six days straight when my dad died. So what is causing your pain; you and Ana fighting?"

"Um . . . no Ana and I are great I honestly don't know think it's just stress got that hearing coming up."

"Oh yeah, for your son right; good luck with that. Don't worry about the crying you can smash Quentin if he bugs you about it and no one else would care." He went in to the stall and I went back to filing, crying silently.

*   *   *

At lunch I had caved and called my Aunt's office to make an appointment for while Ana was at school and told Mama I was looking at something for Mom for her birthday at a store one town over. It probably wasn't smart Dr. Wittson would tell Mom if I didn't go on my own and Aunt Kate would probably say something to Mama if I skipped.

Making the appointment had been easy it was keeping it that was hard; actually for me it was nearly impossible. I paced back and forth, left came back left again, I spun in circles, argued with myself, tried to sit and be patience, stood in front of the door shaking like a leaf until finally Aunt Kate Came out.

"Alex, come in here before you scare someone" She laughed.

I walked in her office and looked around they all looked the same to me other than she had photos of my cousins on her desk.

"You know I can't treat family."

"Uh I know I . . . I . . ."

"Breathe, Al."

"I just have questions."

"I see, but if they are about cutting I think you need to talk to my mother's old co-worker. He is very good; He was good for your mother."

"Which one, Mom?"

"It was JJ; your Mom had her own consoler before they dated."

"Mama actually went to a consoler?"

"Yes lots of them Charlie was the end of a long line of them and the one that she didn't fight. I took the liberty of calling him when Kyle called me to make sure if you didn't call me to call you."

I looked at her "How did you know I would show up?"

"You like your new life more than you like your unhealthy vice."

I blushed.

"Go sit in the waiting room, Charlie will be here any second."

I obeyed my aunt, but seemed to be even more a mess and fell apart sobbing again.

"Tissues Sweetie" An older gentleman asked. He was dressed like he could have worked here; with the white button-up, dress slacks and a sweater vest. But he had just come in from outside. "You have your daddy's eyes."

"Thank-you Sir" I mumbled, I was so use to being recognized for who my parents were and what they had done that I didn't even bat an eye anymore.

"You're welcome, stressful day?"

I shrugged "Not really yesterday was worse, you?"

"My day is puzzling."

I nodded.

"Want to tell me why you're crying?"

I just looked at him.

"Now that, that is your mama's face" He laughed "Charles Cadley but you can just call me Charlie."

"Al-Alexander . . ."

"Alexander Williams; I know, your Aunt said you are having a bad week how about you come in my office and you tell me why your crying."

I nodded and started to shake.

"Hmm I bet if I asked Harold though we could use the office he used for Tina." He spoke to the receptionist she made a call and produced some keys. "Come on you will like this office I use it for all my claustrophobic clients." He lead me down a hall and through a heavy fire door, into a well decorated court yard "This better?"

I blushed "More air no drowning feeling."

"Good, so why are you crying?"

"I . . . I don't know."

"Well when did you start?"

"On and off since last night."

"And what started it?"

I shrugged and showed him my bandaged arm.

"Is that self inflicted?"

I shook my head the "No, the scar yes but the new cut no."

He nodded "So you use to cut?"

"Yes Sir, I haven't in four years?"

"Did you have any consoling before?"

"No Sir, my mother would set it up and I would skip it."

"Your Mama was good at that" He laughed. "Did you cry like this when you stopped?"

"No, I haven't, I haven't cried since I was like twelve."

"How did you get the cut?"

"From work, I work a C.H.T.D.C Mostly in the Self injury hall my boss is Dave Ellsworth."

"He's a good man. Is this the only injury you have gotten since you stopped cutting?"

"No, I get hit, kicked, bite and clawed daily; this is just the first cut. It was made with a broken spoon; I was breaking up a fight."

"Why do you think your crying?"

"I have no clue, I am crying over the dumbest things and it won't stop; and right now I am crying because I can't stop crying."

"Stress?"

I looked at him incredulously "Oh yeah I just adopted two sons one three one six; the six year old I have a hearing to get him out of where I work, I am trying to plan my wedding and the past month everyone keeps asking me if I am cutting or accusing me of cutting. I have D.C.F. watching everything I do with Paul until May and with Anthony until he is out of the program at C.H.T.D.C." I began to cry harder.

"Slow down" He handed me more tissue "It's ok to cry, stress and crying are very normal you sound emotionally exhausted."

"And physically I don't sleep a lot."

"Well no wonder your body thinks it should cry you're overwhelmed, stressed and exhausted. You said you have a three year old?"

"Yes"

"Does he nap?"

"Yes, or he is an . . . oh so your saying I need a nap?"

"Not quite I am saying you need to rest better but mostly I am saying it is kind of the same thing that you are so tired that everything is upsetting and your body is having trouble expressing it because the cutting enabled you from learning how to properly handle unpleasant emotions."

I nodded.

"You are following me right?"

"Yes, sorry I am still dizzy from the concussion yesterday too."

"Well our time today is up but I will see you next week same time."

"Whoa I can't I just told you I have the D.C.F in my life and I don't want them taking my boys away."

He laughed "Breathe, they will not take your kids for seeking help in fact that looks better on their records and they won't know you're here unless you tell them you come here."

I breathed a sigh of relief "Um ok then, I guess."

*   *   *

"Come help us" Uncle Christian called to me.

"DADDY" Paul jumped into my arms.

I sat Paul down and started cramming wood into the furnaces. "What happened? Me again?"

"Me, sorry" Kenny sighed "I thought I had put enough in."

"I hate when that happens; have you guys been outside it is like zero out." I shivered.

"Yeah, I think I got frostbite going from my car into work. Mom is making chicken soup for dinner."

"Mmm that sounds great" I lifted Paul.

"Hey Al are you ok?"

"Yeah, why?"

"You look like death?"

"Oh," I shrugged; I didn't feel like death I actually felt pretty good.

"Dinner" Lorenzo called down the stairs.

Uncle Christian flinched and dropped a log on his foot.

I laughed "Long day?"

"Extremely" He gritted his teeth.

Kenny and I laughed running up the stairs.

"Hi Mom" I hugged her "Ana's eating at her . . ."

"I know she called. How are you feeling?"

"I'm fine, Mom much better"

"Good, go get your mama for me; her and C.J. are in the attic."

"Ok" I sat Paul in his booster seat and took the stairs two at a time running into a large cloud of dust.

"Sorry" A very dusty Nick coughed "The vacuum exploded on me I am fixing it."

"Ok, but its dinner"

"I know."

I took the attic stairs slower in case they were using the punching bag.

"Twenty-two years of crap" Uncle Chris was saying.

Mama laughed "It is not my fault Christian is a pack rat."

"Marc is too, look at this middle school progress reports?"

"Ehm" I tried not to laugh "Mom says dinner."

"Oh, hi Sweetie, how long you been home? How are you feeling?" Mama looked up.

"I'm fine Mama; I have been home about fifteen minutes" I sighed wondering how awful I looked.

"What's for dinner?" Uncle Chris asked.

"Mom made Chicken soup" I answered.

"Mmm beat you down stairs J.J." He took off down the stairs with Mama on his heels.

I laughed so hard I nearly didn't make it back down the stairs.

Uncle Donavan was starting to feel better and was reading the rental adds at dinner.

"Don, are you leaving us again?"

"Never Suo piccolo(his little one) I am home now" He sighed "Or until you kick me out, but I am feeling well enough to go back to my other day job."

"What's that?" Colt asked "I thought you were a speech pa . . . th . . . speech teacher."

"I am but I like to read the news paper too."

"Um ok?"

"He has always had weird hobbies" Uncle Christian shook his head. "He buys and sells rental properties."

"How is that weird?" I asked.

"It's not, just bland, I guess" Mama frowned at Uncle Christian.

"At least it isn't golf like Fred does now." Uncle Chris made a face mentioning their stepdad.

"So, Paul what did you do today?" I changed the subject.

"Ahh" He said showing me he could press his carrot to the roof of his mouth.

"Very nice" I laughed "What else did you do?"

"VACOOOOM go KA BOOOOOOOOM!!!!!" He giggled Nick blushed.

"I saw that maybe Uncle Christian will by a new model now" I suggested.

"Uncle Nick made it KA BOOOOOM because it did eat too many dusd bunnies."

Nick blushed harder.

"I painted you pitures" Paul continued "And Orenzo plays Ants in pants better than Colt!" Paul had finally stopped adding an "S" to Colt's name.

"Lorenzo" Lorenzo whined "Paul L-Lorenzo, with an 'L'"

Paul looked at him like he was nuts and proceed to tell us about playing with Lorenzo and my brothers, Nick and him were reading Mama's newest book. It was called The Christmas Train, the twins were trying to teach him point perspective, and Colt had played blocks and cars with him.

After dinner I checked the chore chart and calendar tomorrow Lorenzo had a physical, it was Thursday the fourth six days until the hearing, Kenny worked eight am to noon, the beasts worked five pm To nine pm, school restarted and Mama had some sort of art gallery thing in Boston.

I bathed Paul and put him to bed he was full of snuggles and cuddles. Then I logged into my college class to work on the paper due Sunday night "Temper tantrums and how to handle them". At nine my little brothers and Lorenzo went to bed. My parents were in the kitchen playing cards with my uncles and Kenny was up in our room with Juliet. Ana came in around nine thirty and flopped down next to me.

"Ugh!" She groaned "I got a 'C' on my last paper."

"I am sorry" I kissed her.

"Mmm maybe we should . . ."

"It's like zero degrees out and Kenny and Juliet are in our room for another hour. And in twenty minutes or the end of that hand" I gestured to the kitchen "Mama and Uncle Chris are going to practice with me for Friday and Saturday."

"Friday" She pouted.

I kissed her again and whispered in her ear "The second Kenny leaves to walk Juliet home."

"I am showering" Ana squeaked, and ran to the bathroom.

"Alexander!" Mama frowned.

"It wasn't me Mama, I just told her I wasn't going to bed yet."

"Mmhmm and C.J. is the king of France, quite teasing your brother's girlfriend."

I barely stopped myself from laughing "Ok Mom."

*   *   *

An hour and a half later Ana was sleeping peacefully fully satisfied but Paul and I were pacing as he screamed hysterically pulling his ears. I was waiting on Dr. Wittson; I had woke him so he was probably walking up the hill instead of riding as he would want to be fully awake.

Mama tried to help me she put ice packs on his little red ears. Finally after what had seemed like hours and was only twenty minutes of Paul crying because his ear hurt and me crying because I couldn't fix Paul's ears Dr. Wittson arrived.

"J.J" Dr. Wittson frowned. "You can't tell me you didn't know the boy has an ear infection."

"Oh I can but I can't prescribe the Amoxicillin or tell witch ear" Mama laughed.

"Yeah, yeah." Dr. Wittson looked like he had not gotten much sleep in the past week.

"Uncle Kyle it hurts" Paul wailed.

"I Know, little man, let me look" He looked in Paul's ears, nose, and throat. "Double ear infection. Tylenol for the fever and I will call the Amoxicillin in to the 24 hour over on Broadway."

"Thank you, Sir" I sighed.

"You're welcome good night" He sighed and left.

Paul and I didn't get to sleep until three; and bless my fiancé and little brother for not killing me; for bringing him up there screaming hysterically like that. I was proud of Kenny at one point he even tried to help.

CHAPTER 3

A LONGER DAY ISN'T POSSIBLE

I had to take Paul to work with me there was no way Mama and Uncle Christian could drag him sick to Boston and Mom was busy today. I had apologized to Dave profoundly but he just told me to shut up him and Paul were going to have fun and watch cartoons all day.

I had Kevin, Kyle, and Jupiter, but I wasn't fully focused.

"You have a weird name" Kevin Said.

Jupiter frowned "My parents work for NASA; my sisters are named Himalia and Lysithea.

Kyle crinkled his nose "My sister's name is Amber."

"ALEX!" Kevin yelled at me.

"Huh" I jumped.

"You're falling asleep in your lunch again."

"Sorry guys; Paul has an ear infection and we were up until three last night. I will clear." I took all four trays up to the return window. Then I took the boys to their classes happy that the seventh grade and ninth grade classes were a crossed the hall from each other. I could have

16

sat in the hall and closed my eyes to wait for them but I was so worried about Paul I rushed straight to Dave's office.

Paul was fine he was talking to Ana and she had given him his midday meds.

"Oh Thank you" I sighed in relief I had nearly forgotten his meds.

"You're welcome, but he is my son too" She laughed at me.

"I know but . . ."

"Hush" She kissed me "Go back to work I will talk to you later nothing bad."

I nodded and nearly headed back to the boys then remembered I was covering for someone in the B-hall and was to spend the afternoon with Genevieve's roommate and some other young lady both in there for anorexia both were fifteen. I read over the charts as I walked, the other young lady's name was Camilla.

I was in shock when I saw Camilla, I think Paul weighed more. She was skin and bones with a dozen different med tags on her left arm and her clothes hung on her as if they were eight sizes too large. "Who's he? He she asked.

"Oh that's just Alex, he is probably looking for my crazy roommate" Latrice clucked her tongue.

"She could same for you Latrice" I sighed. "And as for Genevieve she is probably headed to her counseling session but you should mind your own schedule not hers. You are headed to . . ."

"Group" She rolled her eyes "But we are not a show off level four. Where's Brenda?"

"My guess is in labor; now come on you're going to be late."

"So you're with us today?" Camilla asked.

"Yes, well at least physically I apologize for my own mental state today I was up late my son is ill."

"You have a son, how old are you?" Camilla looked at me incredulously.

"Anthony?" Latrice asked.

"Paul is three and he is sick, Anthony is six. I am almost twenty-two" I sighed.

"Wait you have two sons?" Camilla looked stunned.

"Yes, They were adopted now can we please walk you're going to be late."

"I don't want to go to group the drug addicts wine too much."

I was starting to see Genevieve's complaint and by the look of it so was Camilla.

"I want to go outside I am finally level two. Take Camilla to group and then take me outside." Latrice continued.

"Not happening" I said.

"Fine I am not going, I will go to the time out room first. Brenda would let me go outside."

Camilla looked embarrassed.

"You are going and I don't care what Brenda does, I do my job right" I picked her up kicking and screaming, she could have taught my boys a thing or two on how to throw a fit. "Are you coming or do I need to carry you too?" I asked Camilla.

"Oh no" She followed quickly "I like group."

"Care to explain your med tags?" I ignored Latrice's fit.

She held up her wrist for me to read them, not only was she skin and bones but she was sickly and suicidal too.

"I know I am a train wreck" She smiled meekly.

"I didn't say that and I never would, I just am reading them I need to know some of this at least for today."

*   *   *

I sat Latrice in her chair at group and she had immediately tried to bolt. I sighed and pinned her in the chair, I was almost sure Anthony weighed more. One of the great things about working with the B and A hall kids were they weren't overly violent and had no interest in stabbing me. I kept her in her seat the whole hour and a half. She was disrespectful and annoying but that was about it. I sustained no greater injury than a head ache and as pleasant as it was I would not trade my wild violent group for anything. I took Latrice to the time out room and Camilla to the infirmary and I went to see Anthony.

"Daddy" He Jumped in my arms.

I held him tight and close "Hey, Jared, I am taking him to Dave's office."

"Ok" Jared shrugged, he looked bored the younger girls were painting his nails and doing his hair.

I laughed "In my locker there is some acetone for your make over."

"Thanks" He smiled.

Anthony ran to Dave's office, "PAUL!" He squealed, jumping on to Dave's bed.

"Shh, Sweetie, Paul's sleeping" Ana said.

Anthony started to shake, and then he realized that was all Ana was going to do or say and laid down next to Paul.

"Alex" Dave frowned at me.

"What, he needs his brother, Dave, Paul needs Anthony."

Dave shook his head "Not that, your dripping blood again."

"OOO" Anthony giggled "Daddy swore"

"How do you know I swore" I looked at him "I don't swear in English."

"It's what Uncle Donavan said when Nick ran over his boo-boo leg and he told me it was an ungentlemanly word."

Dave laughed "Got you a smart one there, Al."

"Mmm" I had turned away from everyone so no one saw me crying.

"Dave can you watch the boys, I am going to fix the bandage on my arm."

"Of course what kind of question is that?"

*   *   *

Ana held me tight "Talk to me, Al, why are you crying?"

"I don't know I think I am falling apart or losing it or both or something. I haven't been focused all day; I think maybe I am over tired."

"You think you're tired?" She laughed "I know you're over tired, how did this rip open" She helped me fix the Gauze.

"Oh that's easy I see Genevieve's roommate issues."

"Al" She rubbed my back "What were you doing with Latrice?"

"I was covering for Brenda."

"Oh she's finally in labor."

"Yes, do you know what she is having?"

"I think a girl."

"That's good" I pulled myself together.

"You alright now?"

"I think so."

"How long have you been melting like this?"

"Since Tuesday night."

She nodded and held me tighter "I love you no matter what."

"I love you too, can we get back to the boys now."

"Hush a minute."

"Ok"

"I love you for you no matter what; please don't hide things from me again." She handed me the appointment card for next week's counseling session. "This, I think, is a great idea." She took my hand pulling me out of the locker room and down the hall to the boys.

"Daddy, Mr. Dave says I get to go home again this weekend."

"Yep, level three like Kevin and Kyle, you will come home every weekend."

"Daddy why is Paul sick?"

"He has a double ear infection."

"Oh, You're taking him home huh?"

"Yep, you to dinner and him home."

"Ok" He hugged Ana "Love you Ana." Then he crawled in to my arms I'm ready for dinner."

I looked at Ana.

She shrugged at me. "Love you too Anthony."

I brought him to dinner and then drove Ana, Paul and I home.

"We're home" I called stirring dinner.

"Up here" Mama called from the attic.

One look around the house showed me my brothers were working or doing homework. I found Lorenzo scrubbing the bathroom floor with a tooth brush. "Really" I just shook my head.

"Shut up" He snarled.

I rolled my eyes "I am too tired to even smack the back of your head."

"Orenzo me Antony comes home tomorrow, Mommy says Daddy will bring him home when he comes home from work."

"Uncle Don is crazy this will never work. Paul listen to me L L L Lorenzo not orenzo and th th th Anthony."

I laughed "Come on Paul lets go find Nana and Grandma."

We headed up to the attic and he spotted Nick at the computer desk and wouldn't move until he told Nick about Anthony coming home and then stayed to whine at him about having home work.

"Mom" I called half way up the attic stairs is Uncle . . ."

"We are all up here" She answered. "How is Paul?"

"Fussy and whiny and; giving Nick a nice earful on why Nick shouldn't have home work."

"Good spot for him, it's good for Nick. Come talk to us and help."

I chose a corner and started to help. Uncle Marc had bought new huge plastic storage tubs to replace the falling apart archaic brown card board that use to be boxes for his stuff in the attic; and there was a lot of it. Unlike Uncle Christian's mess down stairs in the room off the studio it was less band and far less of my father's things. There were lots of photos of Mama and my uncles not many of Uncle Marc himself though. I found baby pictures and pictures of Mama and Uncle Chris in foot ball uniforms. I looked at the side of the box I was going through it said "photos and other stuff". My uncle had such great labeling that other stuff could have meant a twenty-four year old tomato sandwich he forgot to throw out. I found a news paper clipping that read "Marc Charles Williams Jr. age thirty-three died November 29th 1996 at 1:04 am. The Officer on seen reported that Williams' crash was due to driving under the influence of alcohol and driving too fast for conditions." "Oh" I said out loud; understanding why Mama and Uncle Chris didn't acknowledge their birthday much. I continued to read to myself "Williams is survived by his five children: Marc 15, troy 12, Michael 12, Christopher James 11, and Juliet 11. He is also survived by his ex wife Juliet Williams 30, two brothers Richard Williams sr. 37 and Brian Williams 28, and both his parents. Ruth and Marc Williams Sr. of Portland . . ."

"Where is Portland?" I asked.

"What?" Uncle Chris looked at me "It is now part of Middletown use to be its own town, why?"

I handed him the news paper clipping "And why didn't Uncle Marc have them fix the typos?"

"Typos?" He quickly skimmed the paper "Oh um I don't know."

"Know what C.J., there is a lot you don't know" Mama teased him.

"Just one of my old football clips, J.J." He winked at me.

"You lie boy" Uncle Donavan laughed only loud enough for us to here.

Uncle Chris handed it back and I put it in the new plastic bin. I found more old photos and more band articles that I had already seen or read. Then I came across an article head line that caught my eye "Crimson Academy Bengals star center kidnapped". I stopped to read it "Crimson Academy's football center and local drummer Juliet Williams was k . . ."

Uncle Chris pulled the clip from my hand "Not this one."

"Ok" I said "Nana played football?"

"My mother?" Mama laughed "No, what are you two reading over there?"

"Foot ball clips, J.J., It was just a typo" Uncle Chris shook his head.

"You lie little boy" Uncle Donavan hissed stifling a laugh.

I began to dig again found one of Uncle Mike's report cards. There was not one grade over C and all the comments said he needed to apply himself. I started laughing so hard I couldn't breathe.

"What now Alexander?" Mama sighed.

"Uncle Mike's sixth grade report card" I laughed harder.

"Now that" Mom said "Is very laughable."

I dug some more and found an old school flyer entitled The Crimson Times. The headline read "Freshman twins upset varsity" I skimmed the article. Sophomores Henry Wittson and J.J. William paired with their brothers, freshmen, Kyle Wittson and Christopher James Williams are unstop able on the field. After they made varsity freshman year Hen . . ." It went on to tell how awesome they were and even more so with Uncle Chris and Dr. Wittson.

"Mama you guys have a lot of football things" I looked up.

"Well we were all state four years in a row" Uncle Chris laughed.

"It was mostly your uncle, I was just a center he was captain and quarter back" Mama laughed.

I dug some more finding old drawings and old photos, I found an old love letter from Uncle Marc to Auntie Kate. Then I found Mama's tenth grade report card her grades were atrocious all except art. The teacher comments were almost as bad and all the same "Violent, lacks effort, self separating, very intelligent."

"That is what happens when you work to support yourself in high school" Uncle Chris showed me his grades were just as bad.

"Wow" I pointed at the teacher comments.

"Yeah, wow fits that."

I pointed at the name on it the year said it was Mama's but they had typed Juliet in the first name slot.

"J.J" Uncle Chris answered.

"What?" She sighed "C.J. I am trying to . . ." She Crashed out of her corner trying to stand up, Uncle Don caught her. "Go finish dinner."

"Oh, Ana's down stairs Finishing it for you" I said.

"Quit laughing, Christopher James" She sighed and scowled at him.

I lifted another school paper it was on School policies. "After the kidnapping of . . ."

"Not that one" Uncle Christian had moved near us when Mama had fallen. "Here read this instead"

He handed me Uncle Marc's senior year book. Mama was listed as a freshman; she was listed and pictured under the art department and the varsity football team. Uncle Marc looked stressed, tired and plain awful; I read some of his comments: "Sorry to hear about your dad.", "Going to miss you next year in college.", "Good luck with your siblings.", "Call if you need any help." They were nothing of the wishes of happy summers and future planes mine held. Someone had written "I signed your crack" In the crease of the book. I looked up "Mama Uncle Marc's friends seemed . . ."

"Supportive" Mom said firmly "Your Uncle didn't go to college right after school."

I found one comment from Mr. Wittson "See you at dinner bro, Mum says don't be late and call your mum—Kork." A lot just offered condolence of him not attending college in the fall or for my grandfather's death.

"Dinner" Ana called up the stairs "And Alexander, go move your car, it has started to snow! Don't you ever watch the news?"

"Oops" I blushed.

"I'll move it" Uncle Christian offered.

"Thanks" I handed him the keys.

"And was it C.J. or I you were looking for earlier?"

"Uncle Chris" I blushed "Dave needed him to fix something when he gets a chance."

*   *   *

Ana had put Paul to bed and was now helping, Mom and Mama, move Uncle Donavan down to the room off the studio. I was laying out clothes for Paul tomorrow.

"Suit him, Lorenzo and I have a will reading in the morning" Uncle Christian and Uncle Donavan were "motivating" Lorenzo into his new room and to finish his school work.

"I don't want to go" Lorenzo whined.

"Why?" Uncle Don frowned.

"We didn't have anything of value" He muttered.

"They will have your clothes you can't where your uniform and Nick's old pajamas around the clock" Uncle Christian sighed.

"I don't have any; I burned them with everything else in that apartment. I hawked what I could and burnt the rest."

Uncle Christian winced "I see anything of value would have been placed in a bank safety deposit like Dad taught us."

"Yeah" Lorenzo snorted "Except money we didn't have that."

"Your mother owned" Uncle Donavan held his breath "A very special necklace . . ."

"I gave Nonni's necklace to Aunt Gabby."

"Ok" Uncle Christian sighed and turned back to me "Then Lorenzo has consoling."

Lorenzo started to object and thought better of it.

"See Don, time and patience, come Alex lets help your mothers move things it's bad form to let the ladies be doing all the manual labor."

Uncle Don snorted "*Your ladies* would smack you for that comment."

CHAPTER 4

FRIDAY THE FIFTH

Ana took her own car to work as she had a doctor's appointment before work and Paul was riding in with Uncle Christian; it made my ride to work rather lonely. When I got to work I rounded my crew up; most were headed home for the weekend.

Genevieve was sitting on top of the book case reading her English book, Sadie and Tiffany were playing cards with Kyle and Kevin, Tiny, Jupiter and Anthony were playing chutes and ladders and the new girls were watching TV.

"ANDY PANDA BEAR!" Genevieve jumped on to Andy's back.

"Ooff my Genie in a bottle you have grown some" Andy laughed. "I am on my lunch I spoke to Mr. Ellsworth and Ana. Ana will be bringing you to me at four."

"Ok" Genevieve said not letting go.

"How are you, Ms. Andy?" I smiled.

"Good and you?" She shifted Genevieve.

"Stressing, how did Ana look?"

"Stressed."

I nodded "Well you enjoy your break I need to greet my . . ." My thought trailed off as I watched Tiffany and Sadie speak to Tiffany's mother.

"Parents" Andrea smiled.

"Yes, sorry" I blinked "Thank-you" I walked over to my mothers and hugged them. "Mom I think I may need your help" I looked over to where Tiffany was now crying.

"No problem" Mom hugged me tight.

"Daddy, daddy, daddy Uncle Christian take Orenzo he can miss today cause the doctor pricked him and the ugly guy in a suit said he might has to go to a d taint mint physical for playing with fire in his old home and Uncle Christian said over no her wont!"

Lorenzo blushed "Shut up Paul! You don't go around telling people that."

Mom dragged Lorenzo in to the hall by his ear.

Paul ran over to Anthony telling him all about his week; the vacuum, preschool, and mostly Lorenzo. Mama had wandered over to Tiffany, Sadie and Tiffany's mom, and blessedly Ms. Meyer's walked in and straight over to the boys.

A man I had never seen before came in and over to me "Hi, the frazzled looking young lady at the front desk said I would find my son here?"

"His name?" I asked thinking the man had the wrong room.

"Jupiter, I see him now he is over there" He pointed to Jupiter "Also his sisters miss him they are in the hall, may they come in they are five and three . . ."

"Of course all family is welcome I am . . ."

"ALEX" Tiny yelled "Anthony and Paul are . . ."

"One second Amelia" I stopped her from yelling "Alex I am Alex" I shook the man's hand.

"You seem very busy I will just get Himalia and Lysithea and visit with Jupiter."

I smiled and went over to Tiny "I was busy Amelia . . ."

"Sorry but they were fighting, no worries though solar system split them up" She cut me off.

"Your taunts don't offend me Amelia, my name is one of honor for I am important to my father" Jupiter

I raised my eye brow "Right, anyway, Jupiter your father and Hi . . . Him . . ."

"My sisters?"

"Yes, sorry."

He smiled "They are named for the moons of Jupiter, my father works for NASA in the research department his primary focus has always been Jupiter."

"Nerd" Tiny rolled her eyes "Al, where is Will and Cart?"

"Here soon I hope" I sighed.

"You suck" She yelled at me.

"In your dreams" I muttered under my breath.

Kyle's mom picked both Kevin and Kyle up, Tiffany's mom left shortly after that in a huff accusing the center and anyone she could think of for Tiffany liking girls. Once Tiffany's mom was gone Mom put both the booster and the car seat in my car and brought Lorenzo home as his mouth had not improved and she was afraid he would be a bad influence on Amelia. I had Genevieve, with Dave's permission, walk Sadie and Tiffany to their room so they could cry without every one watching them. Jupiter played happily with his sisters and my sons. Finally at three Will and Carter arrived.

"WHERE HAVE YOU BEEN, YOU'RE LATE YOU PROMISED, IT'S THREE . . . ." Tiny started to yell.

Cater covered her mouth holding her tight in his arms "Shhh shhh shh" He soothed "I am sorry, my mom took the car for errands before Cart and I were even awake." He smiled at me "Sorry Al."

"Its fine" I tried to smile.

Carter laughed "It is ok dude, you don't have to lie, we know she is high Maintenance."

I nodded high maintenance was an understatement, I had Genevieve take every one who was done with their visits back to their rooms leaving her, Amelia, Paul and Anthony still in the room.

"Daddy" Paul pulled on my leg "Where did lithium go?"

"Lysithea" I corrected trying not to laugh "Went home with her daddy."

"Oh, I get to take Antony home today, Right?"

"Yes."

"Antony, Antony" Paul ran over to him and tried to drag him out the door.

"Paul" Ana laughed "What are you doing?"

"I am bringing my Antony home."

Anthony laughed "Paul we have to wait for Daddy."

Ana lifted Paul "Oh my silly pants, you have to wait for Daddy to be out of work and then he will bring you two home, I will give Genevieve a ride to her Andy and meet you guys at home."

"OOOOOOH" He exaggerated jumping down and running back to the Lego's.

Ana laughed watching him then turned to me "I need to talk to you after."

"Uh oh" I gulped.

"Not bad" She smiled at me.

"Ok"

*   *   *

Home was a zoo! My brothers were fighting so bad I could not tell who was against who or if it was a free for all, there was pancake batter all over the kitchen, Lorenzo was tied at an odd angle off the back porch railing, the smoke detector was going off and papers were knocked everywhere. I set Paul down and shut off the stove and smoke detector; then I opened a few windows to clear the smoke. I took Paul's snow suit off and had Anthony hang our coats and Paul's Snow suit. Then I found the phone that was ringing off the hook more like off the fridge as it was duct taped to it. "Town zoo" I answered untying Lorenzo.

"Alex?" I could hear the frown in her voice for me answering a phone like that.

"Yes, Mama, you named me Alex."

She laughed "Where is everyone?"

"I just go in it's a . . ."

"Zoo?" She offered.

"Uncle Christian's Worst nightmare ever."

"Oh, Boy did they at least leave the house standing."

"Close to fire trucks this time. Where are you?"

"At the E.R. your uncle fell off a roof, again."

"Ok . . ."

"Sorry, your Uncle Chris, he needs a permanent room here with the way he is constantly falling off roofs."

"I figured it was Uncle . . ."

"That's just it though; your uncle Donavan and your mom should be home by now."

"Have you tried their cells?"

"Your mom's is there in our room on the charger she forgot to charge it last night, and I tried Don's but no one answered. What was that crash?"

"I said zoo, Mama, I will try to find them but it is probably just traffic."

"Ok, did Christian start dinner?"

"Uncle . . ."

"No he is here with me, did your brothers start dinner?"

"I know he is Mama, I was trying to say Uncle Christian is going to cry when he sees *his* kitchen."

"Get them tamed Al; I can barely hear you, see you at home."

"Ok Mama."

I put Lorenzo on dinner but unless it was microwavable he couldn't cook it so he was taking lessons from Anthony on how to make apple pancakes. I didn't know what was worse that the twelve year old couldn't follow a recipe or that the six year old could make a perfect apple pancake without any help.

"Daddy," Paul yelled over the fighting "Uncle Christian be mad."

"I know Pumpkin; can you go play in your room until dinner, please?"

"Ok Daddy bye-bye" He ran off to his room.

I looked at the fight they were a ball of arms and legs rolling around the living room and hadn't even notice me or anything else. I called Uncle Marc for help but he was at the hospital with Mama, so I called Mrs. Wittson. "Sam is your mom home?" I asked when Samantha answered.

"Yeah. MOM" She yelled in my ear. "IT'S FOR YOU."

"Real mature" I rolled my eyes.

"So glad you approve" Sam clucked her tongue at me.

"Hello" Mrs. Wittson took the phone.

"Mrs. Wittson."

"Alex, what's wrong? What's that noise, Are you ok?"

"I um could you come over that noise is my brothers."

"On my way."

I let them fight until Mrs. Wittson got there, I didn't know what else to do besides start cleaning witch I did.

"Alex?" Mrs. Wittson called up the stairs ten minutes later.

"In the kitchen" I called back I had been trying to get the pancake off the walls and ceiling.

"What happened in here?"

"I don't know I walked in to this, Mom and Uncle Don are M.I.A. and everyone else is at the hospital."

"Did you ask Lorenzo?"

"Nope, untied him and he swore at me so I put him to work."

"Ok" She laughed.

Lorenzo looked at me "Um how many do I make?"

"Twelve times four do the math" I growled at him.

31

"Fourty-eight" Anthony smiled at me pulling Lorenzo back to the stove.

Mrs. Wittson raised and eye brow watching them fight "So how do your mothers stop them?"

"Grab one and pull but the problem is it takes two people."

She nodded.

"Thanks again."

"No problem" She smiled pulling what had to be either Christopher or Christian's foot. I grabbed what looked like Nick by the waist and pulled hard. Mrs. Wittson had Christopher pinned down and I had Nick pinned tight.

"Now what?" She asked.

"Pray we pulled the right two?" I smile sheepishly.

"I told your Mama she was crazy for wanting all boys."

"No, just crazy for not selling the beasts; I think we grabbed the wrong two or something . . ."

"So what do we do, I let him go he's just going to go back into the mix."

"Al" Ana called up the stairs "I am home. What's all that noise?"

"I kiss my girl for having impeccable timing. Ana, come help us pin Colt they are fighting up here."

Ana ran up the stairs and tossed her purse on the table and pulled Colt off Christian and pinned him. "Auntie I think you can let go of Christopher now" Ana panted.

"NOOOOOOOOOOOOOOOOO!" Nick yelled trying to kick free.

"Oof, knock it off" I growled taking a knee to the stomach. "I get enough of this at work, enough all of you."

"Seriously?" Ana struggled with Colt, "Are you animals?"

"There is a chance of it" I sighed taking another knee to my kidneys.

"Al?" Mom called up the stairs.

"Mom, can you or Uncle Donavan come help us please? QUIT KICKING ME!" I let off a stream of swears after taking a kick to the knee.

"What . . . BOYS" Mom growls and all four of them finally stopped.

I released Nick and Rolled over holding my ribs and stomach.

"Apologize, all four of you, to Crystalline right now!"

"Sorry Mrs. Wittson" They mumbled.

"Sorry Crystalline," Mom shook her head "Thank-you for helping."

"No problem Tina, I don't know what started it Al said he walked into it." Mrs. Wittson smiled.

Mom bent down and picked up a bag of rubber bands "This. Christian, Christopher three weeks grounded one for going into your uncle's stuff and two for that fight and this mess. Start cleaning now!"

"Yes Ma'am" They sulked off her voice had left no room for them to argue.

"And you two" She looked at Colt and Nick "Can go help them, one week for tying Lorenzo to the back porch."

"But Mom . . ." Colt thought it was bright to argue.

"Don't even start; just move your butt your Uncle Marc and your mama called Don's cell as soon as it had reception, the traffic on two is awful near the Glastonbury."

"But . . ."

"Should I make it two?"

"No Ma'am" He whined.

"Mom, I had no part in tying him, in fact I was trying to stop them from that, although I am the cause of the pancake that Al cleaned off the ceiling and why he is currently doubled over holding his stomach" Nick confessed.

"Thank-you for your honesty, but you are still grounded and you are still helping clean."

"Yes ma'am" He went to help the others.

"You ok Al?" She helped me up.

"Yeah just annoyed it was like a Lord of the Flies night mare."

"Dinner" Anthony called.

"Thank-you Lorenzo, thank-you Peanut" Mom hugged Anthony "It is nice to have you back home."

Mrs. Wittson smiled "I will see you later; I left a roast in the oven."

"Thanks again Crystalline" Mom sighed.

"No problem, Tina" She smiled and left.

*　　　*　　　*

After dinner was band practice, Ana played with the boys and my brothers scrubbed everything my parents could think to make them.

"Hault" Uncle Mike sighed "Alex where are you?"

"Here I think?"

"What are you thinking about?"

"Ana wants a beach wedding" I smiled happily.

Uncle Chris laughed, He was fine other than a concussion everyone swore wouldn't affect him because he had no brain to begin with.

*　　　*　　　*

Anthony was up at six the next morning, he woke me. I showered and dressed then had him dress. Then I made breakfast for everyone; Paul was up at seven and up to mischief in Lorenzo's room.

"Up . . . up . . . up Orendzo," Paul sat on Lorenzo chest hitting him with his pillow "You has to get up and get your G on we be late ups Orendzo."

Lorenzo just put a pillow over his head.

"Paul" I laughed pulling him off Lorenzo "Go get Mommy."

"Do I have to get up?" Lorenzo groaned at me.

"Are you grounded?"

"No."

"Then up and at 'em."

He groaned again "What day is it?"

"Saturday, now just get up" I sighed.

I heard my mother's moving around their room and a note I found on the bathroom mirror said Uncle Don and Uncle Christian would be back in time for Karate.

"Morning Mom" I returned to the kitchen to greet her and hand her a plate.

"Morning Sweetie, Please tell Eric that they are all grounded and we will see him next week."

"Ok."

"Oh and your uncle needs your help."

I smiled "I saw the note."

*   *   *

Ana sat with Paul while Anthony had class and I helped Eric; cruelty was I was told to work with Lorenzo on his belt sheet as he was the only white belt this week for his age group. We spared in my class and my uncles watched the boys watch us; well Anthony watched Paul tried to help.

After karate Ana and I helped muck out stalls while the boys played in the snow. Although Lorenzo did not like mucking out the stalls he seemed to enjoy the horses. When we were done mucking stalls we went and got Lorenzo things he needed; his inheritance aside from what he burned down held a collage trust fund and enough money to replace what he burned. He fought tooth and nail on every little thing making me almost tell him he was an ungrateful brat as at that moment my mama was painting a New York skyline in his room as a surprise. By the time we finished Lorenzo had clothes, school supplies, personal hygiene items, and things to amuse himself with, Uncle Christian and I had headaches, Paul was wild, Anthony want to go play with his action figures and wanted to know why he couldn't have gone home with Ana.

When we got back to the house Lorenzo had chores I sent the boys to play and it was my turn too cook.

"Mom What . . ." I paused.

Mama was cooking dinner "It's ok Al I am teaching Colt, go talk to Ana she is up in your room."

"Oh yeah" I said bolting up the stairs I had nearly forgot she had been waiting to speak to me.

"Nana Orendzo has a kating board and a poopie player."

"Oh really, tell me all about it" Mama scooped Paul up in a tight bear hug.

*   *   *

"Hunny" I hugged her.

"Ugh, you smell like . . ."

"Horse I know I am going to shower after dinner" I cut Ana off "Mama said you wanted to talk to me."

"I got my test results back, all negative just cysts."

"That's great news" I hugged her tighter.

She pushed away "Sorry Al but, go bath, YUCK!"

I laughed and went to shower.

*   *   *

Grounded meant that my brothers worked instead of eating junk food and playing pool while my parents preformed. Lorenzo worked too and he hated it, he whined incessantly and my uncle was making me teach him how to bus tables still.

"It's too heavy" Lorenzo said for the three millionth time.

"Quit whining, Ha una targa su di essa (it has a plate on it)" I growled. A hand landed on my shoulder and started to steer me towards the kitchen "Hi Uncle Marc, how are you?" After twenty-one years I was use to my uncle's unique way of greeting people.

"I am tired, it was a very long day. Your son needs you; I thought I told you to get him head phones."

"He left them at home" I walked faster now knowing where I was being directed too and scooped Anthony up.

"Daddy I am tired" He yawned.

"Ok, go to sleep."

"Paul . . ."

Paul was asleep on top of Anthony's blanket and under his own. I carefully lifted Paul and grabbed the blanket. Then I tucked Anthony in and put Lorenzo's head phones, that Uncle Mike had confiscated, on him. He snuggled into his blanket on the edge of the cot.

"Thank-you Uncle Marc" I said and went back to teaching Lorenzo until it was time for me to play.

*   *   *

"I never asked for your opinion, you never offered up a thought. It wasn't like you didn't care you just were never here. You were out with him and I was here alone. I never thought you'd do me so wrong." It looked like Mama was going to cry but the look didn't last, I looked at Uncle Christian and he shrugged.

After that song we switched to the request can there were four for lost soul and three for heart breaker. So we did lost soul. The pool hall was so packed that there was a line outside to get in. the request can filled to over flowing three more times before Uncle Marc said it was inevitable that we had to play heart breaker. Uncle Chris looked like he was in some sort of intestinal pain and Mama groaned; she felt the song was awful and way too much bubble gum pop.

Uncle Marc counted off and Mom Began to sing.

"There goes the heart breaker, blonde hair, blue eyes he's the hottest guy around. Breaking hearts all over town, with just his looks. Lately when he passes me he doesn't smile much."

Uncle Chris gulped and he looked at Ms. Nikki and smiled.

"Oooooooh heart breaker, are you heartbroken. Did someone stomp your heart into the ground to wipe that dazzling smile off your face?"

I don't know if it was a wince or a flinch but Uncle Chris stepped to the left and looked like he just wanted the song to end.

"Give me a chance heart breaker I only have eyes for you. Oooh heart breaker I can put that smile back on your face. Oooooooh heart breaker, are you heartbroken. Did someone stomp your heart into the ground to wipe that dazzling smile off your face? He walks around without a care he doesn't see what he has here. She had him once and it tore him apart left him in heart broken pieces. Oooooooh heart breaker, are you heartbroken. Did someone stomp your heart to the ground to wipe that dazzling smile off your face?"

I sighed and shifted my hands on the drum rest I could see Mama's point about it being bubble gum pop.

"He doesn't see all the girls' giving him attention he's stomping around in that sulky mood. They smell fresh meat and want in on the action, not me I'll wait around for the main attraction."

Uncle Chris visible to more than just someone focusing on him flinched and Ms. Nikki hopped up on stage singing the last chorus with Mom, Uncle Christian and Mama. Uncle Marc Called set break.

"Twenty-nine years later and you still can't finish that song!" Uncle Mike complained once we were out of the screaming crowed and back into the kitchen.

"No, I was fine with the song; open your eyes, Mik. Ok that song isn't my favorite, but if you look you will see that I am pouring blood from my hand, the string snapped against it in the first stanza." Uncle Chris said putting his bloody hand in his face.

Uncle Mike fainted.

"Never could handle his blood" Dr. Wittson laughed. He looked at Uncle Chris' hand "You're fine C.J."

"I know it just hurt like hell for a moment" Uncle Chris said washing his hand and arm.

*   *   *

The rest of the time on stage request seemed to be mostly from younger patrons wanting to hear covers of new bands. We were packing up and waiting on my brothers to finish their cleaning, when a heavy set woman with olive skin and large loose black curls and a thick Jersey accent, tapped Mama on the shoulder.

Mama jumped and swung. "Oh Gabrielle I am so sorry. Are you ok?"

"Fine, fine, my own fault J.J. I know better than to sneak up on you." Ms. Gabrielle laughed "Where is Christian?"

"He's in the kitchen with Don."

"Oh, those two still?"

"Yep, Don's staying with us now. Oh and Gabby this is Alex, my and Tina's oldest."

"Pleasure to meet you Ma'am" I smiled recognizing the name of my uncle Don's on and off girlfriend and Lorenzo's aunt on his father's side.

"He's a dead ringer for Colt."

"He *is* Colt's, Gabby" Mom laughed coming out to the car with Uncle Chris' guitar "Colt Jr. is inside"

"Tina" Ms. Gabby smiled hugging Mom tight "How's Lorenzo doing?"

"Wishing he had gone to you not Christian" Mama laughed.

"Is Christian set on keeping him?" Ms. Gabby looked hopeful.

"I'd say so has him in school, counseling and has already threatened a judge."

"We'll we better go inside before he notices J.J. isn't in there" Ms. Gabby laughed.

I checked on my boys they were sound asleep on their cots, Lorenzo was in a booth half asleep next to Ana whom was asleep. My brothers were taking for ever because they were goofing around with K-4 and Jeremiah more than they were cleaning. Uncle Marc and his family had left earlier as they had church in the morning. I stood near Lorenzo waiting for him to do the right thing on his own.

"Your aunt is here" I sighed when I was sure he was unaware or just didn't care.

"So" He shrugged.

"Not so, get up and go greet your aunt, she drove up here from . . ."

"Trenton I know where she lives!" He muttered a few choice phrases and went to greet her.

I followed because I didn't trust his ability to follow even the simplest of any request or orders given.

"You look tired" Ms. Gabrielle hugged him tight.

"Hi Auntie, I am tired, I worked" Lorenzo whined.

"I bet you do work, your Uncles are hard working family men, I think it will do you some good."

Lorenzo muttered some rather unflattering words about my uncles being good for him and I heard Uncle Don yell from the kitchen to put soap in his mouth.

I stifled a laugh and spared the soap I had done that countless times to Uncle Christian when I was younger "They hear well."

He muttered more and sat near his aunt "Auntie are you here to take me home? I need out of here. I have curfews and I have to work and go to school, and do home work and clean. AUNTIE THEY MADE *ME* CLEAN!" He whined at his aunt.

"No, I brought Christian your school records. We will talk more in the morning Lo-Lo, but you are his sister's son and she wished you go to him."

"SHE HATED HIM!!" Lorenzo screamed and tried to stomp out.

Uncle Christian caught him in a tight bear hug "My sister did not hate me she loved me very much but like you she was stubborn and prideful and we did not see eye to eye on a lot of things. In order to hate someone you have to not care about them in any way shape or form. My sister did not hate me she was very angry with my brothers and I because we only wanted what was best for her and sometimes tried to deiced what that best was especially Don." Uncle Christian held Lorenzo they were both crying.

"Excuse me Mom, Mama we are done now Mr. Wittson dismissed us" Nick tried hard not to stare at Uncle Christian crying.

"All four of you can go wait in the van with Kenny" Mom said "And carry your nephews out to Al's car for him."

"I can do that, Mom" I went to stand.

"So can they, sit down" Mama said.

"Um ok" I looked at Ana.

"I have my niece" Mr. Wittson reassured me.

"Ok" I sat down yawning.

"We can talk in the morning J.J, that boy looks like he hasn't slept in days."

"Months" Mama laughed.

Ms. Gabby raised an eye brow "Months?"

"I work at C.H.T.D.C. from seven until Dave is done with me normally around five—five thirty." I blushed "Its an hour drive each way"

She nodded.

"Are you sure you don't mind waiting till morning?" Mom asked.

"Of course not, Tina I am exhausted, I had a long day myself. Besides I see my pillow over there walking to your van."

Mama laughed "To each his own, Gabby, but you need glasses Don is not that great looking if I had to choose I would pick Christian."

"Colt for me" Mom added.

"Eww Mom gross" I laughed "Way T.M.I. Mama."

"Your father, not your brother and you know that, your dismissed get moving we will see you at home" Mom laughed and swatted me.

CHAPTER 5

TWO DOWN

I woke in pain, my shoulders burned in objection as I rolled them. We had played drum heavy sets the night before and now my back and shoulders were taking revenge. I could feel Paul on my feet and Anthony between Ana and I. I looked at the clock it was six. I groaned four hours of sleep was nowhere near enough I rolled over and tried desperately to go back to sleep for an hour but it wasn't happening so I got up and went to shower. I made breakfast for everyone and was done by nine when Paul and Anthony came down stairs.

"Daddy we is up" Paul called to me.

"You slept in" I smiled.

"Noooo I didn't, Antony did, I was talking to Uncle Kenny he do homework."

"Ah" I laughed.

They ate and went to their room to play while I called every Italian caterer and florist in the phone book. Then I moved on to D.J's, not that I needed one if I asked my mothers and Uncles would have no problem playing.

"It's six months away" Uncle Christian sat next to me with his plate. "Thank you for breakfast. How are you feeling this morning?"

"Sore and tired."

"Why are you up? Other than your children I heard you long before I heard them."

"I couldn't sleep."

"I see; it is warm enough to go the stables."

"Sounds good, but Mom wants me to talk to Ms. Gabrielle."

"Gabby will be up soon."

"Ok" I said and dialed another D.J.

Uncle Christian took the phone "You don't need a D.J. that would hurt your mothers."

"Back up"

"You think we are going to croak that soon?" Uncle Chris sat down.

"Well what if you wish to dance?" I asked.

"You know for a fact that we can work around that just fine Alexander" Uncle Christian frowned.

"Ok, Ok I am just nervous."

"Still?" Uncle Donavan sat down.

"Yes, Sir" I nodded.

"You will be fine" He laughed.

"I can't find a caterer nor um do we have a church?"

"Yes and hush" Mama hugged me.

"Morning Mama" I hugged back.

"Morning, any church will marry you, but your uncles and I got married in the church we grew up in; the congregational on main. Or you can just get a J.P. as she wants it on the beach."

"Oh yeah" I blushed "A J.P. I forgot about those."

"Have you finished your invitation list?"

"Kind of, waiting on Ana to make sure we have every one."

"Ok did you pick a design?"

"Witch ever one Ana wants" I smiled.

"Good morning" Ms. Gabby came up the stairs smiling "J.J. you are wrong he is still my number one pillow."

"Thank-you" Uncle Don smiled like he was a little boy with his hand caught in the cookie jar.

"P.G. room" Uncle Christian turned green.

Ms. Gabby laughed "I saw Lorenzo's room, how do you guys get him to keep it so clean?"

"Nothing special" Uncle Christian shook his head "He just has not had time to destroy it yet or he wants it that clean you know Mio Piccolo . . ."

"Homes are for free expression not good impression" Mama tapped his head with a news paper; "Especially a bed room."

"Al and I are going to take Paul, Anthony and Lorenzo up to the stables and then to Colt's grave."

"Care if we join?" Mama asked "Has been far too long since I visited him."

"Of course not" Uncle Christian smiled.

"Ahhhh" I groaned.

Uncle Christian took the phone away again "You need to walk away for a while now."

"No, I need to find a caterer, for July fourth."

"Still" Ana frowned, "You think that seven month advanced notice is enough for someone."

"Tell me dear" I hugged her.

"What kind of catering services are you looking for?" Ms. Gabrielle asked.

"Italian, but no one is willing to work on the fourth of July even for over time."

Mama laughed "Alex, breath work on your guest list so I can get those invites out."

"I can't decide," Ana blushed "Can we do all three."

"Yes" Mama laughed.

I handed Ana the guest list she added a few names I had missed and then handed it to Mama.

"We are headed to the store Gabby needs a few things we will meet you at the cemetery" Mom hugged Uncle Christian good bye. "And get Al to relax."

"Mmhmm" Uncle Christian laughed "Work cut out for me today. Play with my great nephews, visit my brothers, perform a miracle or two . . ."

"Not funny" Mom swatted him.

*   *   *

"This is *MY LIZZY NOT YOURS*" Paul yelled at Anthony.

"Paul Michael, in this house we share. If you cannot be polite to your brother you can go sit in the car" I frowned at him.

"*But Lizzy is mine*! Nana says dendim *is his*!"

"Denim is his but, you need to share, be polite and be patient" I sighed.

"Daddy, which one is Denim?" Anthony instantly wanted to now.

I looked up I was mucking out Lizzy's stall While uncle Don, Uncle Christian, and Lorenzo were mucking out the other row of stalls. "Denim is in the stall by the door."

My mothers' owned a set of stables. We owned sixteen horses in our stables and rented out the other twenty slots. There were trails, tracks, and training arenas. Also riding lesson, birthday parties and pony rides were available in the spring, summer and fall. It was mostly Mama's business but Mom enjoyed it too. I finished Lizzy's stall and moved on to Cracker Jack's. Cracker Jack was Uncle Chris' horse. Lizzy was a product of Cracker Jack and Butter Cup. Butter Cup was Uncle Christian's horse. By the time I time I got to Denim it was noon. Mama had packed us soup thermoses. The boys sat on hay bales to eat. Uncle Christian got a picture of them playing on the hay bales.

After all the horse stalls were mucked out I taught Anthony how to saddle his horse, climb on his horse, and where and how to hold the reigns. Then I helped Paul on to Lizzy and put both boys on the circular pony track. I went out on my horse when my uncles were done eating and could watch Paul and Anthony on their horses. Once I felt stable again on Thunderbolt I took the boys alternately over the trail once with me.

Thunderbolt a product of Brandon and Emmy which were Mom and Mama's horses; he was a beautiful stallion, with a sleek black coat.

I road right into the stall and hopped down pulling Anthony off "Daddy, do all the horses have names?"

"Yep, starting on that wall Emmy, Brandon, Cracker Jack, Butter Cup" I pointed to the horse as I said the names "Thunderbolt, Hiccup, Coralline, Xavier, Pep'e, Lasso, Lizzy, Denim, Serenity, Black Jack and Lone Wolf."

"That's a lot of horses."

"Yep that is just our horses I don't know the names of all the horses in the rental stalls. Denim is your horse now." I showed him how to lead denim in to his stall and how to comb his hair and braid it, and then I helped Paul bring Lizzy in. I explained that there were farm hands that Mama hired to take care of the horses on a daily basis but if we were coming in they would leave our horses for us.

*　　*　　*

Uncle Christian and Uncle Don cleared off my father's head stone; then I showed the boys. Uncle Christian told Dad about Mom and Mama I told him Ana said yes.

We got home around four thirty my brothers were outside playing in the snow Lorenzo joined them happy to be free of my Uncles.

"Daddy I stay with Uncle Christopher" Paul said.

"Um hold on" I sat Paul down to talk to my brother. "Christopher can you watch Paul for me, Ana is still out with Mom and I have homework and cho . . ."

"We will . . ."

"Gladly watch . . ."

"Them," The beasts shrugged in unison "They . . ."

"Can be on . . ."

"Our team."

My sons were brave and ran right off to play with my brothers. I went up stairs and did some home work and some laundry. Then I sat at the table; Ms. Gabrielle was cooking something that smelt really incredible. Uncle Don had said that Ms. Gabrielle was staying until Thursday which was good because I still hadn't had a chance to speak with her per my mothers' requests.

"Thank you for setting the table" She smiled at me.

"You're welcome Ma'am" I answered.

"Always so formal and uptight; sweetie, just call me Gabby. How about you tell me about your boys?"

"Um ok Ms. Gabby."

She shook her head "You got your father in you."

"Thank you Ms. Gabby."

"Give it up Gabs, that boy still calls me Sir" Uncle Donavan laughed.

"There isn't anything wrong with manners" Uncle Christian glared at Uncle Donavan.

"I would too you are frighteningly ugly with all those bruises and unappeasable, and perpetually crabby on a good day. I on the other hand can be quite sociable." Ms. Gabby swatted him.

I stifled a laugh.

"I can't be that ugly my daughter is gorgeous" Uncle Don retorted.

"And she looks like her mother" Uncle Christian end that debate "Now look you went and confused Al."

I blushed "No I know who Jasmine is, geese my memory isn't that bad. I was trying not to laugh"

"You fools go I am trying to talk to him" Ms. Gabby shooed them.

"Good luck" Uncle Christian laughed "He's only after your Pollo parmigiano (chicken parmesan)."

"Shoo" She swatted me "Get out of that it's not ready yet; now tell me about your children."

I laughed "It smells incredible" I thought about my boys "Paul is three and Anthony is six and the adoption was final the beginning of December."

"Tell me about Anthony, your mother says you have a hearing on Wednesday and your lawyer isn't available so you had to pay for someone else."

"Yeah the center's lawyer is sick so we had to go with the cheapest we could find; the guy is a real tool and looks at Ana like she wouldn't even comprehend anything he says."

"What's the hearing for?"

"Anthony, to get him out of C.H.T.D.C."

"Why is he there?" She looked back at me from dinner.

"Foster care caught him cutting three months, well almost five months ago now; wow that went fast." I shook my head. "Anyway the state placed him in there and when I adopted the boys the state said he had to complete the program. But he is smart and tough he is already a level three."

"He is too young for the state to classify him for self injury even if it is true, they should have gotten him a therapist first whose laziness was that?"

I blinked "Um, their worker now is Ms. Meyers but before it was some guy I didn't really interact with. And Dave said he was too young that's why Dave is helping me fight it."

"Is it too late to change your lawyer?"

"No Ma'am."

"Just Gabby" She shook her head "Cancel the 'tool' and tomorrow bring me with you to work."

"Pardon"

"I am a lawyer sweetie"

"Oh"

"Sorry, I thought some one told you"

"No ma'am, I don't stay still long enough unless my mother's or uncle's need me too."

"Hunny, I know what they do," She laughed.

"Yeah", I sniffed in the oven again.

"Shoo, it's almost done."

I pouted.

"Hush or I won't make manicotti tomorrow and your uncles will cry."

I laughed Uncle Christian loved manicotti. "Shall I call everyone in?"

"Yes please, so that they will be in and ready."

I ran down the stairs to the porch and called "Ora di pranzo (Dinner time)!"

*   *   *

"That boy learns slowly." Ms. Gabby shook her head.

"I warned you." Uncle Donavan kissed her cheek.

"I meant Lorenzo, and don't you start that, you chose a long time ago."

"I can't change my mind?"

"MMM" She glared at him. "You still chasing down old ghosts?"

"Not lately, I've been here."

"Because you hurt yourself so badly, chasing down that last one." Uncle Christian chided.

"Hmm, Jasmine graduates this year" Ms. Gabby glared at him.

"I know, I call her daily, Gabs, I am very proud of her" He tried to kiss Ms. Gabby's cheek again.

"We will talk about your mind later" She swatted him away blushing slightly.

"Um" I cleared my throat.

"Sit" Uncle Christian said.

I obeyed.

"Your Mama has your invitation list, and you and the boys had tux fittings?"

"Yeah, kinda."

"Kind of?"

"The guy called he needs the boys back closer to the wedding especially Paul. So I set it the Monday before the wedding."

"Ok you have a reception hall?"

"Yes, Ana asked her Uncle . . . ."

"Oh that's right and you have a band did you get a J.P.?"

"Yep Ana did that."

"And the florist I did so I didn't hang you, what do you need?"

"A CATERER!"

"Alexander" Mama frowned sitting at the table.

I stood and hugged her "Sorry Mama."

"You didn't speak to Gabby yet?"

"I did I have to call Mr. Whatever tomorrow and fix him."

"Ahh" Ms. Gabby Said.

I opened my mouth and she shoved a bite of food in my mouth. "Mmmmm"

"That's better" Ms. Gabby soothed "Now stop your fussing and call them in again because it's getting cold."

Uncle Christian laughed.

"Don't you laugh little boy, I will set you straight too. Al has a lot of Colt in him."

"Until he is sick then he is *all* Tina" Mama laughed.

"You will caterer for him right? "Uncle Don asked.

"Of course, and miss a chance to dance with you? Never" Ms. Gabby laughed.

*   *   *

Dinner was incredible; I played with the boys until their bed time. Ana put them to bed while I canceled the lawyer instead of waiting until tomorrow; then went over the case with Ms. Gabby. Dave and Anthony would not need to be at the hearing. She went over my adoption papers making copies of everything.

"Ma'am may I ask something unrelated?"

"Gabby, just Gabby and of course you can."

"I um Ma'am are you married to my uncle?"

"Oh good lord sweetie no" She laughed "That man is too wild to marry."

"Er oh" I looked at Uncle Donavan asleep in his news paper."

Ms. Gabby looked too "Ok eight years ago he was untamable. Maybe now at fifty-three he is less wild but those injuries . . ."

"Oh so your dating?"

She laughed again "I wouldn't call it that we share a child and a good time when he shows up."

Uncle Don snorted "Only women I ever loved."

I laughed.

"Love, that's what you call it, fine we will go with love then" She laughed.

At ten I went up to the roof "Talk to me" I said to Ana.

"He's worried I won't love him if he is here every day."

I held Ana close and tight rocking her. She was shivering so I put my sweat shirt on her. I was warm myself till I sat down on the snow. I just held her and looked at the stars. I had no idea what to say.

"I want the song my parents had."

"Um ok . . ."

"Same as your parents!"

"I was three, forgive me forget."

"Sorry I snapped" She started to cry again. "It was 'You're my Best Friend' By Queen."

"Perfect" I kissed her.

"Honey . . ."

"Hmm" I closed my eyes kissing her deeper holding her closer.

"Ehm" Uncle Christian cleared his throat.

I jumped back turning fire engine red "Sorry."

"MmHmm, although you are of age and I would love more great nieces and nephews; I do not wish to see how they are made nor does your son."

I blushed harder coming back inside the attic and taking a tear streaked Anthony from him "What's wrong?"

"I had a bad dream" He sobbed.

I carried him down to his room and rocked him back to sleep then went back to my bed. The note on my pillow said "Sorry dear if Uncle Christian hadn't stopped you I would have, wrong week." I blushed and curled up near Ana whom was sound asleep.

CHAPTER 6

FAST FORWARD

Monday was long and a blur; Anthony went back and it made him and Paul Whine. Ms. Gabby spoke to Dave, Anthony's therapist, and teacher. My day was a blur of miserable teenagers mostly Brittany and Curtis.

Tuesday was just as fast and just as painful. Brittany was nothing but negative attitude and spent the day pushing Buddy and Curtis' buttons until they snapped. Tiffany was so annoyed she asked to go to her room after school. Tiny just tried to attack her. I had a huge bruise on my face that looked like Ana had smacked me with a two by four.

Wednesday morning was such a mess that I grabbed Colt's tie instead of mine; consequently I was being strangled. The hearing was not the pretty or explosive things you saw on T.V. It was actually rather bland and boring, everything was about settling out of trial; I sat staring into space while the lawyers spoke. The mediator asked me a few questions directly mainly about my bruised face.

"Mr. Williams you are aware your son is fully aware of his actions and can clear define and describe his actions?" The mediator asked me after reading the reports from the center.

"Yes, Ma'am, Anthony is very smart."

"You are aware that if he starts to injure himself after he is in you care he will have to return to the center regardless of age?"

"Yes Ma'am"

"Sir, you are aware of how badly bruised your face is?"

"Yes Ma'am, I work at C.H.T.D.C. some of the young men there had a bad week."

"Mr. Williams has your fiancé ever struck or physically harmed you in any way."

I thought I heard my uncle and Ana stifle laughs.

"No, Ma'am" I choked trying not to laugh.

The state's lawyer spoke up "How is that relevant to this hearing?"

"Every time I have seen Mr. Williams he is bruised or bitten. If there is spousal abuse it is your responsibility to find out and remove both children from that house."

The states lawyer looked at me. "We are, all for the child only having to be at the center for therapy, but can Mr. Williams and Miss. Wittson truly handle his needs. My client informs me that although they provide a loving and more than suitable home for Paul, Anthony requires more attention and both Mr. Williams and his fiancé work long hours at C.H.T.D.C."

Ms. Gabby cut in right there "My Clients have two jobs both with extremely flexible hours. Their boss at their primary job at C.H.T.D.C., David Ellsworth, has stated in his report more than once that he is more than willing to give them any and all time off that they need. He also states that my clients stay off the clock to give their sons equal quality time. Both boys once completely in my clients care will be attending their grade school Alma matter Crimson Academy. Paul is already in rolled to start the spring preschool program in February. Arrangements have also been made for Anthony and my clients have paid for a private tutor from the school to go to Anthony five days a week so he gets the education level they feel he deserves. Despite the fact that, the center already works with Crimson Academy for most of their school instructors. Both boys have horses at Rainbow stables and will be taking lessons in the spring. Anthony is enrolled in the local kempo karate studio and Paul will be joining as soon as he is old enough. My clients have followed the adoption agreement to the letter."

"How is Anthony doing all these things from inside of the center?" The state's lawyer asked.

"The minor in question, Anthony Robert Williams, is a level three in the self mutilation program at C.H.T.D.C.; this entitles him to go home between eight am Friday and eight am Monday as a way to help him readjust into his family's routines out of the safety and shelter of the C.H.T.D.C." The mediator read aloud looking annoyed with the state's lawyer. "Ms. Wittson in your opinion how is your son adapting?"

Ana smiled I could tell she was nervous by how tightly she was squeezing my hand. "Anthony does great he loves his uncles and grandparents, and most of all being back with his brother. He is your average six year old; he loves to play, hates bed time, he is full of energy, very inquisitive . . ."

"How does he respond to punishment?"

"I have yet to meet any child who likes time out but Al and I have only had to give him one time out. He had a rather large tantrum over returning to the center and swung at me. Al sat him in time out and then spoke to him about why hitting was unacceptable. It's our three year old that lives in time out. He is definitely three; 'no, mine, you can't make me, I hate you, go away'" She laughed thinking about Paul.

"How did Anthony respond to the time out, Mr. Williams?"

"He screamed and cried telling me he hated me, he hated Ana, he hated every one. He was very tired and cried himself to sleep in the car and woke up in a much more agreeable mood, happy to see he was in my group."

"My client wishes to call a five minute recess" The states lawyer asked.

"Recess granted, oh and Jules the ladies in the hall is out of order use the one near the main court room on the second floor."

"Thank-you Ma'am" Ms. Meyers said.

I stared at the ceiling; this felt hopeless and definitely was not going well. Ana's grabbed my hand again and I remembered I was not alone, it helped a little.

"Mr. Williams are you ill?" The mediator asked when the recess was over.

"No, Ma'am"

Do you realize how pale you are?"

"Sorry Ma'am I am tired."

"Most parents are. Mr. Landow is your client ready to resume the hearing?"

"Yes Ma'am" He answered.

"Good, is your client willing to agree with the wishes of Ms. Lucia's client requests?"

"We wish to add a condition of our own, Ma'am, that they wait until the child is a level four and then start with a two week transition trial as Mr. Williams and Miss Wittson new when they adopted the minor in question my client wanted him to complete the program."

I thought I heard Uncle Christian laugh having the same thought I had; "Dave will fix that."

Ms. Gabby looked at Ana And I.

We gave slight nods.

Ms. Gabby raised and eye brow at me then looked at the mediator "My clients agree to the terms."

"Then there is no need for this to go to trial, it is final upon full agreement of both parties that the minor in question be returned to his parents at level four, for a two week trial at the end of which if the minor has not harmed himself he need only to go once a week to C.H.T.D.C. for therapy and will remain permanently in his parents care."

I let out the breath I had been holding.

*   *   *

Once in the Parking lot at the car I held tight to Ana and explained to Ms. Gabby why we weren't worried about the D.C.F.'s terms. Then I called Dave.

"I am busy and your son is fine, why must you interrupt my manicure?" He answered.

I laughed "We just got out of the hearing."

"I know Jules Called me, you and I will talk tomorrow."

"Ok, thanks Dave."

*　　　*　　　*

"Daddy!" Paul jumped in to my arms "You're early."

"I am" I set him down "I need out of my suit though."

"OOO K" He giggled.

Ana picked him up and dance with him. I took a picture and then headed upstairs to change. Mom knocked on my door.

"Come in" I called.

"You ok Al? You didn't greet anyone." She asked.

"Oh sorry, Mom" I hugged and kissed her cheek.

"It's ok, Sweetie, just worried."

"Oh no, I am fine you know me, can't stand my suit and tie."

"Ok, sweetie, see you down stairs?"

*　　　*　　　*

"When do I get my grandbaby?" Mama asked.

"When he is level four" I laughed hugging her.

"Ok" Mama looked at me "Are you ok?"

"Yeah, just frustrated."

"Wedding stuff?"

"Yeah florist" I had Paul and a phone book on my lap. "The one Uncle Christian had called, called back and cancelled."

"Don't worry you will find one."

"Mama what's that smell?"

"Manacotti."

"OOO" I whimpered "Uncle . . ."

"Gabby, she loves to cook."

"It smells incredible."

"I know" She laughed "Have you seen your brothers? They should be home by now."

"Um I saw Nick and Colt pass about an hour ago."

"Ok I will go check, I know Lorenzo is in his room Don is helping him with his science" Mama headed up stairs.

"So glad I am not in that room."

"I will second that" Ana sat down next to Paul on my lap moving the phone book."

"Ooof" I shifted "Paul, Grammy named me Alexander not Alexandria."

"Ana laughed "He loves you."

I hugged Paul "Daddy loves Paul too."

Paul turned away from his cartoons and looked at me "I wants a sisser."

"Um ok?"

"I wants a sisser so I can protets her like Uncle Christian protets Nana."

Ana started to gush.

I laughed "That's my boy, you're going to be tall and strong like Uncle Christian and I."

"And if I have a sisser her Barbie dolls could need restuing from my ire tucks" He pointed at the commercial for Barbie dolls."

I laughed "We will see about the sister I can't just buy them at the store but maybe if you're good we will get a Barbie next time we are at Wal-Mart."

*　　　*　　　*

"Thank-you Ms. Gabby dinner was incredible." I cleared my plate and several others.

"You are welcome" She said "You know Alex, I have two jobs, I am not just a lawyer . . ."

"Ok" I smiled, I didn't want to be rude but I had band practice and I was tired.

"Do you even read the business cards your mama draws?" Uncle Donavan muttered.

"Not really . . ."

"Hush Don, I am trying to speak to him, Alex I am Caterer also." Ms. Gabby cut me off.

"OOO how much and can you please, please, please?" I begged.

"Your girlfriend hired me on Monday" Ms. Gabby laughed.

"Phew" I blushed "Thank you Ma'am"

"Uhg boy, I will not feed you, it is just Gabby" She shook her head at me.

"Yes Ma'am . . . I have band practice" I flew down the stairs to avoid getting swatted.

"Told you" Uncle Don laughed.

"Told me or not that boy is all Colt" Ms. Gabby shook her head again.

"Nay, he has a lot of Bella in there too."

"Let's hope so according to that report his son is a mess."

"Report's nothing but a pile of ten dollar words. The boy functions just fine now that he is here where he is wanted and loved."

"Mmm."

*   *   *

Uncle Donavan and Ms Gabby were curled sound asleep on the couch when we came up stairs from practice.

"That I like to see" Uncle Christian smiled.

"And you don't think he would like to see you happy?" Mama shook her head at him.

"I am happy Mio Piccolo" He said with a slight pained sound.

"Ok Pinocchio" She laughed hugging him.

"Sono felice. (I am happy)" Uncle Christian repeated hugging Mama tighter.

"Uncle Christian, who is the only women you will ever love, it is Mama isn't it?" I asked.

"Your mother Al, that is all you need to know, I will not tell you which one."

"Mama?"

"Don't look at me, he has never told either of us. I thought he was after C.J. for a long time."

"Really?" I laughed.

"Really but not like that, I thought he was after him to hurt him."

"Oh."

"MMM, you were a very distrusting child, Mio Piccolo" Uncle Christian smiled at Mama pulling Mom into his arms.

"Like Kenny?" I asked hoping they were tired enough to actually answer me.

"No di . . ."

"That one's ok" Mama Laughed.

"Yes, like Kenny, that boy gives me gray hairs" Uncle Christian laughed.

"No more than the twins give me" Mom laughed kissing Mama.

CHAPTER 7

IS IT BED TIME YET!

"Talk about asinine, he won't be level four until the end of May." Dave said "This is not Jules' doing, I hope you know that." Dave shook his head Thursday at lunch.

"I know she didn't say anything other than to excuse herself to the restroom."

"I will push this . . . ."

"Dave, it is fine, just when Anthony is level four make sure those . . ."

"You know I will." Dave shook his head.

I had told him everything and he was not pleased with the state, and I wanted nothing but to let him sit and cool off; he had strong beliefs about D.C.F. and the state of Connecticut.

He dismissed me and I went back to work; I had Jupiter and Genevieve. Jupiter was reading one of Kevin's National Geographic magazines and Genevieve was at group for another half hour.

"Alex do you have scars?" Jupiter asked.

"More than I could count" I looked at my arms.

After few minutes he said "Alex?"

"Yes," I sighed "You know you could just ask me everything at once."

"Uh sure, how many times a day did you cut?"

"A day or in one shot?"

He raised an eye brow "Um both . . . I think."

"I started cutting at nine, it was one cut every once in a while at large pride functions, concerts and things like that."

"I started at eleven in middle school."

I smiled "By middle school it was all pride events, the pool hall, family events and two or three cuts at a time by eighth grade it was school too and four at time."

Jupiter raised his eyebrows.

"By fifteen I was up to twenty or forty cuts a day four or five times every time I cut." I lowered my upper arms so he could see the scars, and showed him my scar that went from my elbow to my wrist. "At sixteen I hit rock bottom. My brother told my Mama and this scar is why he told and looking back he saved my life."

"Oh" He looked at the bright blue band aids over his gauze pads and stitches "It wasn't a cut."

What was it?"

"Ten stabs."

"Well" I nodded "That would do it."

"It was a bad relapse."

"That happens."

"I made Dad put me in here; he didn't want to he felt I would have been fine with just counseling."

I smiled "You have a good dad."

"He does his best, Mom left us after the girls were born for an astronaut. Do you think Dad will forgive me for being undependable and unstable?"

"I would hope so but that's a question for him."

"That's what Jared said"

*   *   *

At six I clocked out and laid down in the time out room. I had not slept well and had no clue why. I laid in the time out room for so long it was forever or more like felt like forever before Ana called to me through the door. I opened it to let her in.

"No you come out, it's time to go home, It is six-thirty" She laughed "Give me the keys and go tell Anthony good night."

I handed her the keys and went to Anthony.

"Why can't I go home yet?" He whined.

"The hearing agreement was that you can come home at level four."

He made a noise of displeasure and started to cry . . ."

"I am sorry but this is how life works."

He had started to throw a tantrum.

"Anthony" Ana tried "At six years old we are too old for temper tantrums. We don't have to like the rules but we do have to follow them. Throwing a fit will not change things, just get you in trouble. You will have to sit in the time out."

It didn't help, I had no patients for tantrums, never had for anyone else's, but my mothers both said I could definitely throw one. I picked him up put him in the time out room and sat in Dave's office for six minutes.

"What are you doing?" Dave startled me.

"Disciplining."

"I mean in my chair, you know better." He shook his head at me "Besides I already spoke to Ana."

"Oh, yeah sorry" I got up and moved.

"You look like hell; do you know you're still just a kid?"

"Tell my body that it forgot to sleep."

Dave Laughed "Well get some sleep tonight."

"Right, I have total say in that."

"Don't you start with me" He stared me down.

When the timer buzzed I went to the time out room door Anthony was balled up on the floor crying. I went in "Time up you're too old for temper tantrums." I took him to his room "I love you, I will see you tomorrow and you will come home until Monday. Good night go do your home work."

He hugged me still crying.

*   *   *

At home Paul had decided there would be no better day to act out and was screaming high pitched shrieks in time out. So I didn't interfere "What . . ." I mouthed to Mom.

She showed me perfect bite marks on Uncle Don's Ankle.

"OOO" I nodded.

She held up Orajel.

I shuttered and nodded.

Ana sat at the table and ate dinner while she read; she was reading a new fantasy series. I sat and ate, while I worked on my poetry. When Paul got out of time out he greeted Ana and then me. He wandered off up the stairs and I found him in my room on Kenny's bed jumping.

"Excuse you?" I tried not to laugh.

"Hi Daddy."

"Get down, you don't jump on beds, why are you up here alone."

"Jumping on the bed. Duuuuhhhh."

"You don't tell me duh, come on it is bath time anyway."

"No I don't want too!"

"It is not a choice."

"I DON'T HAVE TOO!"

"Time out" I lifted him and carried him down to the time out chair and set the timer for three minutes.

"I hate you, Daddy" He yelled.

"That's nice, I love you too."

"You're stupid."

Mom grabbed me and pulled me out of the kitchen "Don't argue back."

"I wasn't, I was getting a drink."

"MMM" She looked at me "Do I want to know?"

"Paul?"

"Yes, Paul."

"Caught him upstairs in my room jumping on Kenny's bed and when I told him it was bath he got mouthy."

"Bad form Paul" Mama said passing through to go down stairs. "That is four in one hour."

"Wow" I sighed "I'm sorry."

"Why" Mama laughed "He is normal, the twins spent almost all of three in time out."

"As did you and I" Uncle Chris laughed he was watching some cop drama show.

*   *   *

After I put Paul to bed I went to bed. Unfortunately I did not fall asleep no matter how hard I tried. At ten when Ana came up I was laying upside down off the side of the bed.

"Hunny?" She laughed.

"I can't sleep, I have no clue."

"Let me try and help."

She crawled into my arms "How's that?"

"Much better" I cuddled her soon she was asleep, but I was still wide awake. I tossed, turned, shifted, flopped, blankets on, blankets off; but nothing helped. At five am I turned off the alarm, showered, dressed and downed three quarters of a gallon of orange juice.

"Wow" Mom laughed "You ok?"

"No sleep" I yawned.

"I can tell."

"MMM, vampire caffeine" Mama looked at me "No sleep?"

"I tried honest, but . . ."

"Shh" Mama laughed "Call the gallon yours we are headed shopping anyway."

"Thanks" I don't know why Mama called orange juice vampire caffeine, I had never asked.

"Hmm . . . someone is sick or didn't sleep" Uncle Chris said.

"Exhausted" I sighed.

"Forget to sleep."

"Tried to sleep."

I woke Paul and helped him get ready to go. Ana came down yawning. Paul and I greeted her after she got out of her shower. She looked at me and shook her head.

"That bad?"

"Bags under your eyes."

"Great and the state lady is there today."

"Fuss later."

I looked at the clock "Yep, bye Mom, bye Mama, see you later I pounded the bathroom door "Have a good school day, Nick"

I heard bottles hit the floor and him yell several impolite words out at me.

I laughed scaring Nick awarded me the twins' approval and four displeased looks from my parents. Ana didn't look impressed either.

"What?"

"You don't normal do things like that."

"A little bird told me Nick has some interesting bathroom shower habits that are making him late to breakfast every day. So I just wanted to see if he was telling the truth or if he was just being slow and whinny."

"And was Colt right?"

I laughed "I'd say so."

"Do I want to even know?"

"No" I laughed "Definitely not."

"Oh! Oh, gross Al."

I laughed harder "I told you."

Paul tore off through security wearing house keys and overalls, again!

"Sorry" I called chasing him.

"Sorry" Ana said trying to help me, catch Paul.

"Mmhmm" Harry said more focused on the non employees.

I caught Paul half way to Dave's office I sat on the floor wheezing and laughing. Greg Chuckled he gave me my inhaler and Paul a lolly pop. "Good work little man, next time try to get to Dave."

"Don't encourage that" I threw my inhaler back at him.

"Oh no this little guy and I have a deal."

"Greg" Ana frowned.

"Oh don't cluck that tongue at me, miss thing anything he does to slow the parents down helps me."

I shook my head.

"Happy Friday" Dave laughed taking Paul and helping Ana Pull me off the floor.

"Mmhmm, I . . ."

"You have your son . . ."

"No I assume you're taking Paul for a bit?" I cut Dave off.

"Yup."

"Ok."

I gathered everyone Jupiter was looking green and shivering, Kevin and Kyle were chatting excitedly Genevieve was in a book, Tiny was as always so *happy* to see me, even more *happy* to see the new girls still in our group. Tiffany was not shy about expressing opinion on Sadie leaving, as Dr. Wittson had finally had time to review what Dave had sent him and felt regular counseling would be fine for her and had contacted her parents and they were coming today to get her.

Anthony tugged on my leg "Where's Paul?"

"Huh, oh, with Dave" I yawned.

"Daddy what's that sound?"

"My cell phone, hold on dear." I stepped away from the racket of the girls and answered "Willams."

"Alex, it's Charlie you missed yo . . ."

"Oh sorry."

"Next Wednesday?"

"Ok. I am at work so . . ."

"I know see you next Wednesday at five."

I hung up; I groaned at the girls and separated them "You guys need not fight, you are all in here, all with me, and whether you like it or not you're going to behave." I had just enough time to take a calming deep breath before greeting Ms. Meyers.

"You look tired" She smiled

"Nope, just settling an argument" I smiled.

"Where's Paul?"

"With Dave . . ."

"Ah yes their count down."

"Yep."

She walked over to Anthony and I sighed in relief.

"It will get easier or more routine at least. Are the boys ready?" Kyle's stepdad tried to reassure me.

"Yes they are and they are quite excited" I smiled.

"You alright you look awful."

"Fighting girls" I yawned.

*　　　*　　　*

No one was happier after lunch in fact I think they were more miserable. Paul was still a bit whinny from his ear ache and Genevieve was impatient with the other girls. Amelia who didn't have patience to start with was pushing my patience. Jupiter was still green but was playing with his sisters and again I thanked my parents for a normal name. Tiffany was holding Sadie and screaming at Brittany. Lynn was watching TV.

"Oh Alex, you look awful today" Andy came in.

"Thanks Ms. Andy" I laughed.

"ANDY let me go to work with you please! These immature brats are making my head hurt!" Genevieve jumped onto my back from the top of the book case.

"Ooff, glad to be your ladder" I laughed.

"Actually, when you're done abusing him I was thinking dress shopping and dinner out with Pauline and Rochelle."

"OOO" Geneviève jumped off my back "I'm ready, we going to the steak house or . . ."

"The steak house yes and dress shopping for their wedding this Sunday."

"Oh I remember they are going with blues. Bye Dog breath, see you Monday." She grabbed Andy's hand and pulled her out the door.

I laughed and turned into a frightening looking women and a scared looking man. "You must be . . ."

"DADDY!" Sadie hugged the man.

"Sadie's parents" I smiled.

"And who are you?" The lady asked.

"Alex Williams, Ma'am" I gulped.

"Good I was supposed to hand you this."

I read the note from Ana and pulled Tiffany out from under the couch.

"You have excellent control of them last time Sadie was at a place like this the kids were running wild."

I smiled trying not to laugh "Thank you Ma'am but it is not me half the kids have gone home already, two are mine and well don't get too close to the other girls." I laughed nervously.

"Hello Mrs. Ebren" Tiffany mubble.

"Hello Tiffany, I almost didn't recognize you without your make-up."

I waited nervously for Dave, Tiffany not letting me walk away from her and she wouldn't leave Sadie. Amelia and Brittany were glaring each other down and Lynn was playing with my boys, Jupiter was more green and reading to his sisters.

"They seem to like you" Mr.Ebren said.

"That's a first" I sighed "Tiffany I need to check on Jupiter he looks really green."

"The planet's fine" Tiny called to me I think she was enjoying my discomfort.

I sighed "Thank-you Amelia" I gritted my teeth "Please stop calling him Planet and or solar system."

"Something you wish to say?" Sadie's mom asked her after the fourth time Sadie opened and closed her mouth.

"I am sorry, I didn't tell you" Sadie squeaked.

"That's fine, I knew, I meant to Tiffany."

"Oh, I already said sorry to her . . ."

"I meant like see you next Friday?"

Sadie blushed "Oh um yeah I . . ."

"Her mother already called me."

My eyebrows shot up and I looked at Tiffany.

"I told you so" Tiffany shrugged at me. Louder she said "I am sorry about that Mrs. Ebren."

"Not your fault, Sweetie, so how long have you two been dating?" Sadie's mom asked.

"You're not mad?" Sadie gulped.

"Why would I be mad, how many times must I tell you, you can tell me anything I love you."

"Three years" Tiffany blurted. "I love her."

Sadie dived behind me.

"Sadie" Mr. Ebren frowned "Don't hide that's something to be proud of there are marriages that don't last that long."

Sadie blushed.

"Sorry Al" Dave saved me "Buddy started a fight with Curtis."

"When doesn't he" I sighed "Dave, this is Mr. and Mrs. Ebren."

"Nice to meet you" Dave smiled "If you will follow me I will get her belongings, they are all packed, and I will let you meet her consoler and you can take her home."

Around three Will got there, Brittany was standing Whining at me about her dad being late. She looked Will up and down and let out a soft whistle; that was enough to send Amelia over the edge. Amelia sprang off the couch and dove at Brittany.

"HE'S MINE!" Tiny shrieked along with a string of profanity.

Will caught Amelia and I moved Brittany.

"I am yours only yours, well Carter's on . . ." Will started to sooth her.

"T.M.I." I laughed.

"I was hoping she would laugh," Will rocked her, "She is always so sure I am going to leave her."

"See you guys Monday morning"

"Monday Al" He carried her out. Dave was letting her go home for the weekend to see if it made her more pleasant to be around.

"Alex I don't feel well" Jupiter finally admitted after his sisters left.

"I will call Greg, hang in there."

He nodded.

Tiffany and Lynn were playing with Paul and Anthony. Brittany was back in her room, and Jupiter was in the infirmary. I took the thirty seconds to blink, bad move on my part. Lynn took it as a signal that it was ok to put Tiffany in a head lock. I looked at Anthony but he just shrugged.

"Dave" I sighed into the Walkie-Talkie.

"Do I want to know?"

"No."

"You sound like you're battling orangutans" Dave laughed.

"Non così divertente, Dave (Not funny, Dave), so far from funny. Tiffany . . ."

"Breathe Al; I am already half way to you."

I couldn't breathe I had been hit in the stomach hard enough to knock the wind out of me but I had succeeded in separating Lynn form Tiffany's head.

"Really" Dave said to me taking Lynn.

"I took a minute to blink, I am sorry" I wheezed.

"What caused it?"

"I don't know I blinked."

Dave looked at Tiffany "You swing first?"

"Nope was playing with Al's son" Tiffany shrugged.

"Well, um, ok" Dave shrugged "It is four Al, so you know what to do."

"Yup see you Monday." I took Tiffany to counseling, signed Anthony out, grabbed ours coats and my check and met Ana at the door.

"You boys look cute" Ana smiled up at us.

I had Anthony on my shoulders and Paul in my arms "Let's go home I am tired and hungry."

"You're always hungry" She laughed.

"I am hungry, too" Anthony said.

"You didn't eat lunch" I told him.

"It tasted bad, I like Nana's cooking."

Ana laughed.

*   *   *

"Steak, veggie, mac 'n' cheese and baked apples" Mom said "Your brothers are working or doing homework."

"Grandma" Anthony came in with Ana after they stopped at her dad's.

"How are you?" Mom hugged him.

"Hungry, like Daddy and I am home."

She laughed "Your daddy is always hungry."

"That's what Ana said." He looked at me.

"I am; look at the size of me takes a lot to energy to keep me going."

"Then lay off the junk food" Mama stretched up and thunked the back of my head.

I laughed and hugged her "More like café food at work."

"Can't be any worse than your Uncle Mike's cooking."

"Oh yes it can" Ana said "Well taste wise no, but nutritionally yes, it's all salt and empty calories."

"Something taste worse than today's lunch?" Anthony looked scared.

"Many things" I laughed.

"Daddy where's Paul?"

"He's out back playing in the snow."

"Can I go, too?"

"Of course just get your snow stuff on."

"Dinners at six" Mama said.

"Dad what time is it?" Anthony squinted at the clock.

"It is Five thirty."

"How long do I have to play?"

"A half hour."

"Ok" He belted out the back door and down the stairs.

The back yard wasn't big it was fenced in and the only gate opened from the outside. Uncle Marc said it was fenced in because of Uncle Chris trying to jump the cliff just pass the fence. Uncle Mike said the fence never stopped anyone.

I checked the chore chart and did my laundry and cleaned the bathroom in my and Kenny's room; he had left tooth paste all over the place again. I did my online class work and looked over Paul's week of pictures and things.

Lorenzo looked awful at dinner.

"Lor . . ." I went to ask.

"Floor scrubbing" Uncle Donavan said "Never killed you."

"I was just going to ask how his day was" I said.

"It sucked the teacher is a . . ."

Uncle Christian covered Lorenzo's mouth before he could finish "It is unbecoming of you to use such ignorant and unpleasant language."

Uncle Chris snorted stifling a laugh.

"Hush C.J." Mom said trying not laugh.

"Yeah" Mama stifled a laugh.

Uncle Christian shook his head at them "Colt how was your day."

"Fine I guess, some girls were checking me out in lunch until I tripped and fell face first in my salad."

"OOO" Nick grimaced.

"Not your best moved" Mama agreed.

"Alex how was your day?" Mom asked.

"Way too long, the girls were all fighting, that new one is an instigator and Amelia won't quit calling Jupiter planet and solar system."

"It was like state worker malfunction day at the front desk, it was a line of confusion." Ana added "And there was a fight in the A hall that was really bad."

I grimaced "Was that Curtis and Buddy?"

"No, one of the kids there and Joan; broke Joan's nose."

"Oh not good" I shook my head "How was your day Nick."

"Good, lacrosse practice starts soon Uncle Joe says he will help me; and Mags asked me to the Sadie Hawkins dance next Friday."

"Did the Twins say if they are going?" Mom looked at Mama.

"No, but their attending is behavior dependant" Mama sighed "How was your day C.J.?"

"Pleasant a lot of weather proofing and installation; we live in New England you think these people would not wait for January." He laughed "Oh well more work for me, what did you do today Don?"

"I was lost without Paul" He laughed "I read the real estate there is a decent condo complex out in Manchester for sale. Figure I'll clean it out and up and lower its rent."

"Bland" Uncle Christian laughed.

"Bland? Ok house wife what did you do?"

"I cleaned stables and ran beautiful ladies around to where they needed to be and we also grocery shopped" Uncle Christian said proudly.

"E io sono blande, Soccer Mom (And I am bland, soccer mom)?" Uncle Don teased "How was your day Paul?"

"I went to Daddy's work. D—all and I added another Band-aid to the shart for Antony come home. I played cards and Lego's and hugged lystintia and Dupider turned geen and, and Sadie's girlfriend say 'Oh nos you don't'" He did the head and body swish.

I nearly spit my milk.

"To rittany because *me* Den Ovieve said she was being hadeful."

Mom laughed "Well you had a busy day?"

"His speech is getting better I could actually understood half of what he said" Colt laughed.

"Daddy, may I be excused?" Anthony showed me his empty plate.

"Clear your plate" Ana smiled.

"He is ready to be home" Mama made a face.

"Not according to D.C.F." I sighed.

"Don't get discouraged" Uncle Chris said.

"It's frustrating."

Ana rubbed my back "We aren't giving up, it won't take much longer he is doing great."

*   *   *

After the boys were in bed I had band practice and Ana watched. Uncle Chris had picked this week's sets and next week we would go back to Fridays and Saturdays.

"I think we need to talk and you know it's true you be . . . . Mike must you make snoring noises?" Uncle Chris scowled at him.

"Yes, yes C.J. I must! That song was Awful in 2002 it's awful now."

"Fine! What song do you want?"

"I don't know."

"Then don't complain."

"Well then sing on pitch."

"ENOUGH, you sound like little kids" Uncle Marc shook his head.

Uncle Chris started again "You weren't here so you never knew all the feelings I hid from you, then you came back in like you own the place and I should bow down to you . . ."

A basket of dirty clothes landed on Uncle Mike's head.

"Ooops we're . . ."

"Sorry Uncle Mike." The Twins ran down the stairs quickly picking up their mess.

Mama and Uncle Chris were laughing.

Mom on the other hand was not "*Boys*" she said sternly.

"We slipped on this . . ." Christopher held up a lighter.

"Honest Mama" Christian took his dirty boxers off Uncle Mikes ear and a sock from his shoulder.

Uncle Chris took the lighter "This isn't mine" He passed it through the room. No one could claim it. This would be bad when band was over.

"BOYS!" Mama yelled.

Or now I breathed in, it was never good when Mama yelled like that; the studio was sound proof not Mama proof especially, with the door to the house open. All of my brothers and Lorenzo made it down the stairs in record timing.

Mama held up the lighter "Whose . . ."

"Thanks Auntie" Lorenzo took the lighter "I've been looking for that; good thing, I was afraid Paul would find it."

My mothers looked so angry I thought he wouldn't live, but it was my uncle that spoke "You are more than lucky your cousins found it and not Paul or your aunts." Uncle Christian took the lighter "In this house children under the age of twenty five do not get lighters without special permission and at twelve I find no reason for you to have a lighter. You are grounded bed immediately, thank you for your honesty."

Lorenzo opened his mouth to argue but Kenny grabbed and pulled him up the stairs, before he could say anything.

Ana looked at me, I was still holding my breath.

"Al, it is ok to breath" Mom said.

"The pyro had a lighter" I gasped.

"Technically Al, he isn't a pyro his moment in New York was out of extreme mental anguish and duress" Uncle Don said.

"Bull . . ." Uncle Christian switched to Italian and nothing appropriate for the human ear.

"Christian!" Mom frowned.

He had been speaking so low and so fast I had only heard the first string of profanity.

"Am I wrong?" Uncle Christian asked.

"He is your nephew" Mom frowned again.

"Nephew or not he is still an ill mannered unstructured beast!"

Mama signed "Time and love Mio Roccia"

"Break I need a walk" Uncle Christian sighed.

"I shall join you" Mama took his hand and Mom's.

"I have . . . bo . . . ok Chris . . ." Mom spluttered.

Uncle Marc laughed "Have a good walk Tina, the boys are fine."

Ana laughed and dragged me up the stairs.

"Whoa girl" I laughed.

"Kenny went out with friends your parents are out and our kids are asleep."

"Um . . . OH ok."

CHAPTER 8

SATURDAY JANUARY 13TH

"Ouch . . . Ouch . . . Ouch . . ." Ana was combing her hair. "Would you let me" I offered, I was eating breakfast. She blushed "Seeing as you are the one who tangled it?"

"Not intentionally." I blushed so hard I choked on my coco pebbles.

"OOO Al . . ."

"Is blushing . . ."

"He must have . . ."

"Got lucky." The twins teased.

"Daddy what does Uncle Christopher mean?"

"Ehm" I blushed harder "Nothing, he's teasing me, Anthony is your Ghi on."

"Yes, but Paul won't give me my belt."

Ana looked at Paul and laughed "Paul" She frowned trying not to laugh harder "Please give your brother his belt."

Paul had the belt wrapped around his face and was walking around like a mummy. I laughed and pulled the belt off his head. Anthony took it but stood like he was waiting to be yelled at or worse finally he just told Paul to go get dressed. Lorenzo was loading all the gear into the van and my. We were headed to the stables after karate and my mothers were not. My uncles were arguing over sports and my mothers were motivating my brothers.

I smiled at Ana.

"Yes" She looked up at me.

"You're pretty."

"Dork" She laughed "Paul tell daddy he's a dork."

"Ork" Paul giggled.

"Ok, ok I'm a dork but she's still pretty."

"Daddy?"

"Yes, Anthony?" I answered.

"Why are you a dork?" He crinkled his nose.

"Because I was staring at Ana with a dopey grin."

"Oh why?"

"She's pretty."

"Oh" He looked lost.

"Ameal E a says that a ork is a whales . . ." Anthony covered Paul's mouth and pulled him down the hall to their room."

"Leave him breathing Anthony" I called after them trying not to laugh so hard I stopped breathing.

"That" Ana swatted me "Is exactly why they are too young to be there" She bristled down the hall to tell Paul there was more than one meaning for certain words.

I just laughed so hard I choked on my breakfast.

*   *   *

My focus at karate had been nil, I could hear Paul in time out. He had been spending a lot of time in time out. Mama said it was normal, but I didn't know how much longer I could handle it before I snapped. It was like he was purposely trying to push buttons for fun. I ended up taking several well placed kicks from Kenny during sparing.

At the stalls Ana was helping Anthony brush Denim and I was helping Paul with Lizzy, when it started small, small drips. I left Paul and went looking.

"Al? What's wrong?" Ana asked.

"Don't you hear that?" I was looking everywhere.

"Hear what?"

"Ana this is more a house than a barn it has a kitchen and bathroom, it is heated and above all else my uncles rebuilt it five years ago it doesn't leak. Don't you hear the drips?"

"All I hear is my son singing to me."

"I heard drips, is it raining?"

"Al, it's still snowing."

The drip . . . drip . . . drip . . . drip turned to a drip, drip, drip . . . drip, drip, drip . . . drip, drip, drip . . . drip, drip, drip.

"Tell me you heard that, Babe."

"Heard what Al?"

"There is a leak somewhere."

"Al, what are you doing?"

"Calling my mom" I paced in a circle "Yeah Nick put Mom on . . . . Mom there is something leaking here . . . ok . . . ok . . . drip, drip, drip . . . yeah fast like that . . . yeah hose and faucets off . . . ok . . . ok . . . no . . . ok thanks Mom." I hung up.

"And . . ." Ana looked at me like I was crazy.

"She is sending Uncle Chris."

"Ok."

I went back to helping Paul, I could hear Anthony singing to the radio; but I could also hear the dripping. After ten minutes of waiting the drip turned to a drizzle."

"What's that?" Ana asked.

"Now you hear it? That is what I was talking about."

"That can't be good."

"Nope"

"What do you think it is?"

"Last time it was half frozen pipes."

"Mommy looks Lizzy pitty." Paul called.

"Uh oh" Anthony hid behind a hay bale.

"Huh?" I looked; Paul had poured a whole bottle of horse shampoo on Lizzy and turned her pink. His very patient horse was just looking at him chewing her apple. I had to look at the ceiling so I didn't start laughing and failed laughing anyway.

Anthony peeked out from the hay bale.

Ana laughed "Paul, Lizzy is all soapy now."

"Lizzy pitty, Mommy, pink" He giggled.

"We have to rewash her now silly."

Anthony came out and watched. "He's not in trouble?"

"He has to replace the shampoo with his allowance but other than that there is no need to punish him more" Ana hugged Anthony looking at me worriedly over his head.

"Anthony how about you help Ana clean up Lizzy and Paul can help me find that leak" I smiled hoping that would help.

"Um ok" He gulped.

"Ana don't turn Anthony pink" I laughed she had that devilish glint in her eye and her hands full of pink soap bubbles.

"Turn me pink" Anthony squeaked.

"Soap foam, Pumpkin" Ana laughed throwing a handful at me.

Paul giggled grabbing soap foam and putting it on Anthony's head.

I shook my head laughing as Ana turned both boys pink with soap foam. I went to search the pipes. The drip had switched again from the drizzle to a drrriippp run dripdripdrip drrriippp run. I heard my Uncle's truck pull in.

"In the kitchen, Uncle Chris" I called out.

"I figured" He shook off snow.

"Snowing again?"

"Nope, it has stopped just slid off the roof on me."

I laughed.

"Hush, have you found the . . ." Water poured on his head "Never mind."

I stifled another laugh.

"Don't you even dare, just call my sister."

"On it" I burst out laughing unable not to laugh at the sight of my drenched uncle. "Colt put Mama on." I sighed waiting for Colt to listen. "Pipe burst on Uncle Chris' head" I laughed harder, when Mama got on the phone "Sorry Mama I know the pipe busting isn't funny, yes Mama, ok I will" I hung up. "She is sending Uncle Mike."

I helped him pick up the shattered pipe pieces. Uncle Chris took his shirt off and hung it to dry "At least it wasn't hot water."

"MMM" I agreed "That would have hurt."

"Hush you" He shook his head. "Why is that horse pink?"

"Paul."

"Again that's the fourth time this week!"

"I know he is replacing it."

"Not what I meant, I mean I am starting to fear he thinks the horse should be pink. I fear at like twelve he will spray paint the horse."

Uncle Mike laughed

"Like you and Uncle Rod's head?" Uncle Chris greeted Uncle Mike.

I had never met my great uncle Rodney but I had met our cousins Ricky, Mitch, and Rodney Jr. Mama never had anything nice to say about her uncle.

"I am not admitting anything; I am still pleading the fifth" Uncle Mike laughed setting a ladder up "Alex you know Paul's horse is half pink."

"Yup, Ana and the kids were fixing that when the water main blew."

"Well I am working on it unless C.J. wants another ice shower, I had to cut the water off till it's fixed . . ."

"But there is still more in the pipes" Uncle Chris waved him off helping me clean the water mess on the floor.

"For what they pay the stable hands . . ." Uncle Mike muttered to himself as he worked.

Ana was toweling off the boys from their soap foam fight, so they could play on the hay bales.

Uncle Mike fixed the pipe in an hour and in two hours we had Lizzy back to her proper color, dried, brushed and happy in her stall.

*　　　*　　　*

I plugged my ears Lorenzo was singing rap music loudly as he scrubbed the bathroom floor. "You learn slow, very slow" I sighed. Paul and Anthony went to their room to play and I flopped down to watch TV.

"Don't sit on my couch wet" Mama frowned.

"I'm not wet" I laughed "But Uncle Chris might have hypothermia."

"I do not, that is not the first time I have come home in the middle of winter with no shirt."

"Let's just hope this time it isn't because you were necking with some girl and rolled in horse poo" Ms. Nikki laughed.

Uncle Chris blushed "Never Baby Doll you are the only girl I ever did that with, my shirt's in the wash pipe burst over my head and the little thing on the couch there just laughed like a hyena."

"Poco (Little)?" Uncle Don towered over him.

I started to laugh again.

"Enough you two" Mom separated them "Al, hush he gets enough of that from your mama and uncle."

"Thank-you Tina" Uncle Chris blushed.

Ms. Nikki handed him a clean shirt "You look ill?"

"I think we need another practice before tonight" Uncle Chris made a face.

"I was thinking that too" Mama nodded.

"Mmm definitely" Mom added.

"Meet you down stairs" I sighed.

"Don't want to play?" Ana kissed me on her way up stairs with our laundry.

"I do I just don't think this song is going to get any better."

"Having trouble?"

"Not me; Uncle Mike, doesn't like the words."

"Oh."

"Taking the boys with me."

"Fine, I was going to play cars with them" She fake pouted.

"Ok, that's fine too."

"No, let them decide."

"Ok" I laughed, I checked the chore chart on the way and I had vacuuming tomorrow and dishes on Wednesday. "Boys?" I opened their door.

"Just me Dad, Paul fell asleep in his toy box."

"Awe" Ana rushed and got a Camera before I moved him.

"Ok, well, Ana and I had wanted to know if you wanted to stay up here and play cars or something with her or come down and watch me practice."

"Can I please stay with Ana we can play the mouse trap game Uncle Kyle got me for Christmas."

"OOO dang and I have practice; you have fun and save me a game, mouse trap is my favorite."

He looked at me odd then smiled "I like connect four best."

"Ok I will see you at dinner time."

"What is dinner?"

"I don't know the calendar said eating out."

"Cool!"

*　　　*　　　*

An hour and a half later we had it nearly perfect, the song had been in limbo a long time according to Uncle Chris and that's why it had not been on an album.

"You didn't ask so I didn't answer, you weren't here so I didn't bother. Time went fast moving slowly, I found out that we needed to talk and you know it too. Every night I lay awake listening for you to come in, you don't even bother to come tell me good night anymore. You are up and out the door before I am even awake to avoid confrontation."

I kept up with the beat this time.

"You didn't ask so I didn't answer, you weren't here so I didn't bother. Time went fast moving slowly, I found out that we needed to talk and you know it too. For someone who loves me you're never around. For someone who cares when I need you most you can never be found.

You didn't ask so I didn't answer, you weren't here so I didn't bother. Time went fast moving slowly, I found out that we needed to talk and you know it too.

Day in and day out we go about our lives not crossing paths avoiding the signs. You say you love me, can't live without me, want to walk me down the aisle. Well I got to tell you it's time that you hear that thoughts that I have cause You didn't ask so I didn't answer, you weren't here so I didn't bother. Time went fast moving slowly, things grow apart left for the lonely. Offers arise that one can't deny so it's time that you hear me once and for all baby I love you dearly, but Darling, Dear, Honey Bear hear me clearly step up or step out simple as that step up or step out no more ifs and or buts step up or step out.

You didn't ask so I didn't answer, you weren't here so I didn't bother. Time went fast moving slowly, I found out that we needed to talk and you knew it too."

Uncle Donavan nodded "Molto buono, piccolo fratello(Very good, little brother)."

"Thanks" Uncle Christian smiled like a little boy who had just been told he was cool by a big kid.

*   *   *

The pool hall wasn't too packed the sleet outside was probably what was derailing customers. Ana was teaching the boys to play pool and I was warming up. Uncle Donavan was irritating anyone too close to the bar, although he called it bar tending.

"DAAAAAD" Jr. and Adam came flying in "Dad, Uncle Kork call nine one, one some dumb . . . some guy just hit the tree on the corner."

Uncle don called 911 and Uncle Marc, Dr. Wittson and I ran out to the crash. A car full of teenagers had hit the tree; three of them had crawled out and were panicked. Uncle Marc and I went to the two in the car; the driver I wasn't about to touch, the passenger in the back was stuck and panicking. I went to the side not smashed to the tree, cut the seat belt off him, and helped him out as the sirens went off.

The driver was severely stuck I opened the passenger door and tried to talk to him. "Calm down, take a deep breath, hear that siren we called for help."

"I'M STUCK!" He screamed.

"Stay still, talk to me, what's your name?"

"Devon; I can't feel my legs!" Devon screamed again.

"It's going to be ok Devon."

"I'm a good driver" He cried.

"Ice, does every one in."

"Are you a Wittson?"

"No a Williams, Alex Williams, but Dr. Wittson is right here."

"No, no tell K-4, Devon's here" The boy passed out, probably from the pain and panic.

I went to stand with my uncles as the EMTs and ambulance pulled up. We waited as they checked the kids. The first three were ok just rattled and a few bruises but were fine. The fourth one was taken for a concussion and Devon was taken on a stretcher but they said he would be ok just needed X-rays. The police said that the ice must have panicked them when they hit it. Other than that they weren't speeding all were wearing seat belts, just young and new to ice.

We all went back inside, I told K-4 what had happened seeing as it seemed important to Devon. That made K-4 happy. I raised an eye brow at him.

He laughed and ran off to do dishes.

"It is his chem. Lab partner . . ." Christian said.

"His sister is smoking hot." Christopher rolled his eyes.

"She has an uptight daddy . . ."

"You want her you have to . . ."

"Be in with her daddy and Devon" Both of them rolled their eyes looking unimpressed.

"All air and high maintenance to me" Adam muttered on his way to the kitchen to get more deicer.

*   *   *

I flopped on the bed face down Ana rubbed my back "It wasn't too bad."

"I fell face first in spilt food" I groaned.

"It wasn't like everyone saw just Sam and I."

"I have ketchup in my hair."

"Oh you'll live, you big baby."

I rolled off the bed and hit the floor "I . . ." I fell asleep.

CHAPTER 9

BOOGEY MEN GET SLEEP, DADDIES DON'T.

"Off" I groaned Paul lifted me by my hair.

"Hi Daddy, why you on floor?" He yawned.

"Um I don't remember, I think I fell asleep here." I looked at the bed Anthony was in my place next to Ana sound asleep. I could hear Kenny snoring. "What time is it?"

"Hero, tree, one, two" Paul proudly read my digital clock.

"Three twelve, Paul, why are you up?"

"Boogey man."

"The Boogey man isn't real"

"He's in Antony's bed" Paul was frantic.

"Ok, ok I will go look" I lifted Paul so he stopped trying to pull me up by my hair and took him down to his room. He was right someone was in Anthony's bed but it wasn't the Boogey man. Next to the bed was a back pack with the initials D.J.W. "That's not the Boogey man, Paul, that is just my Uncle Danny" I tucked him back in "It is Nana's little brother, he must have gotten back from Russia early."

Mama's younger half brother, Danny, was seven years younger than her. He had sandy brown hair, bright blue eyes, and a goatee. He wasn't as tall as Uncle Jesse, Uncle Tim or Uncle Troy but he wasn't as short as Uncle Mike and Mama. He had been touring Asia; he traveled a lot with his job, something to do with solar paneling and "going green". Mama said the planet had been trying to "go green" since she was the beasts' age, but I think it was just now finally happening even if she felt it never would.

"Lots of uncles" Paul yawned.

I laughed "Yeah, I know, we have a huge family."

"Is he scary?"

"No, just snores and sleeps a lot."

"Ooo" He giggled "Night Daddy, I loves you."

I slogged back up stairs.

"Daddy is that you?"

"Yes, Anthony."

"Daddy it is really dark walk me down to the potty?"

"There is one right here in the room" I walked him to the bathroom door.

"It's ok Daddy you can go back to standing by the door."

"I was . . . never mind" I went to bed and pulled Ana in to my arms, five minutes later Anthony pulled us apart pulling one of my arms and one of Ana's over him.

I must have fallen back to sleep no problem because two hours later I woke with a start shaking. I checked the clock it was five twelve a hole whopping three hours of sleep. I quietly went down stairs to check on Paul. He was fine sound asleep, Uncle Danny as predicted was snoring.

Lorenzo met me in the hall "Who's the chain saw?" He yawned.

"My Uncle Danny" I sighed too tired to correct him on being rude.

"Ugh" He went back to his room.

I went to the living room, Kenny's iguana was walking over the bests' boas' cage I sighed again and put the lizard thing back in its tank. I curled up with the dog on the couch, falling back to sleep.

At seven thirty something landed on my back "This I believe is yours" Uncle Danny said groggily.

"Daddy" Paul giggled "He makes funny noises."

"Sorry Uncle Danny" I mumbled.

"It's fine I am sure my sister and brothers have spoiled him not to mention Christian."

"Mom and Uncle Donavan too."

"I bet see you at noon, I got in around three."

"I know, you scared Paul"

"Sorry about that, good night."

I groaned and remoted the TV on to preschool cartoons and on auto pilot poured a bowl of cereal and plopped it and Paul at the breakfast bar, then grabbed a cup and the half empty carton of orange juice. I looked at the cup then the juice and then the cup again. I put the cup back and just downed what was in the carton; then propped myself against the breakfast bar near Paul.

"Daddy you look BAAD" Paul smiled at me.

"Thank-you Paul, I didn't sleep well" I yawned.

"OOO, Daddy let's play Ooties."

I nodded "Ok" in my mind I knew how to roll a dice.

Around nine Mama came out of her room "Wipe the drool dear before you slime the cootie" Mama hugged me.

I looked up "Oh um yeah he wanted to play."

"He is winning; you have your tongue in the foot hole."

"He's a Picasso cootie" I yawned.

Paul giggled "That's what Uncle Chris says."

"That's what he use to tell me too. Oh Mama Uncle Danny is home came in around three last night scared Paul."

"That boy" She shook her head "I told him not to go to his old room."

"How long is he here for?"

"I don't know he didn't say."

"Nana, Nana, play with us?" Paul begged.

"After I eat, dear" She hugged him.

"OK; Daddy are you home today? Can we go sledding and play play-dough and paint and play cars and Daddy . . . Daddy are you listening? Daddy . . . Daddy . . . ? Nana he's night-night and the sun is ups."

"You pay him no mind, go get Uncle Christian and Grammy."

"Otay" He raced in to Mom's room.

"Al . . . AL . . . ALEX . . . ALEXANDER JOSEPH!"

"AHHH" I jumped "Sorry Mama, where's Paul?" I put the cootie pieces in the box.

"Fine, doing me a favor and then making his bed."

"Sorry."

"Go back to bed."

"Nah Ma . . ."

"Alexander, I said go back to bed."

"Yes, Mama" I snuck down to the studio and started to play.

"Che non è letto! (That's not bed)!"

Paul bee-bopped down to the studio and started to play his drums too, it was a fisher price my first drum set, it had been mine. He had no rhythm, but I didn't mine I laid my head on my drum set and listened to him play after a while he went up stairs and I started to play again. Ana came down stairs doing the boys laundry. I fell into a steady beat watching every one go in and out, until I was too tired to play and passed out on my drum set.

*　　*　　*

"Dad . . . DAD . . . DADDY!"

I jumped and fell off my drum stool.

Anthony looked down at me, Paul next to him.

"I think you brote him" Paul said.

"Did not, he did that himself, Dad Ana wants you, she said Grandma wants you."

"Ok" I slung Anthony on my back and Paul up in my arms and carried them up stairs.

"Sorry . . ."

"Al . . ." The twins panicked when they saw me.

"Che(What)?"

They held up one of Paul's toys "We will . . ."

"Replace it . . ."

"Next pay day . . ."

"What, oh don't worry about it, where's Mom?"

"In . . ."

"Her room."

I carried the boys to the living room and then went to my mothers' room "What's up?"

"Want to catch a concert?" Mom Asked.

"Um sure which one?"

"Stomp"

"YES!"

"Go tell the others."

"And no more passing out in the studio, it's not safe" Mama added.

"Yes Mama."

My mama had been telling me not to pass out in the studio since I was in high school. It never was intentional to pass out down there; the studio was sound proof, as little kids we weren't allowed down there alone. Now we just had to tell someone we were down there.

Stomp was my Mama's favorite to watch or hear however you viewed it. We hadn't been in two years tickets were expensive and sold out fast. Mom had probably pre order in November. Lorenzo sat in between Uncle Christian and I, he looked like Uncle Christian had fed him poison. He grumbled all the way there and through to intermission when he fell asleep. I thought my uncles were going to kill him.

"Let him sleep, he and I will speak later" Uncle Don said "Suo Piccolo(his little one) and Bella should be allowed to enjoy this.

CHAPTER 10

MONDAY THROUGH FRIDAY

The week that followed was a blur of no sleep and work. The girls were no happier this week than last week and the stomach bug that Jupiter had caught was now going around. Ana and I worked hard not to catch it.

Monday although Jupiter was better, Tiffany and Tiny were sick. Brittany was stuck in her room other than meals until she could behave. Lynn was quite without Tiffany to harass, Anthony was mad at me for bringing him back. Kyle and Kevin were ok until Buddy harassed them at lunch and Genevieve was tired.

Tuesday I was tired and filling in, in the C-hall. Buddy and Curtis took turns terrorizing me and each other, by the end of the day I had new bruises and a head ache.

Wednesday was mellow, by then Jupiter, Anthony and Genevieve were the only healthy ones in my group, and Thursday was similar. Thankfully they were well behaved aside from some generalized complaining about cafeteria food or having to be there.

Home was slightly less exhausting. Paul was still practically living in time out, but I had lots of pictures to look at that he drew for Ana and

I. Uncle Danny was still home, but was working or sleeping. Therefore no one saw him much. Ana was just as tired as I was as her nightmares were keeping her up, but she didn't tell me what they were about. I tried to ask everyone every chance I got something about Mama's past and got a lot of time with Uncle Marc telling me to knock it off.

Friday was the longest day all week, Ana and I were both tired and Paul was excited to have Anthony back. I rounded every one, all finally healthy again, up and instantly they started to fight. Kevin's and Kyle's mothers met us outside the family room and I was ever grateful. Anthony and Paul went right for the Lego's. Genevieve joined them; Andy had called to say she'd be late. Tiffany was pacing the wait for Sadie was making her nuts; Lynn teasing her about it was not helping. Brittany and Tiny were at each other's throats, I was almost positive Dave gave me both of them for his amusement.

"Morning Alex" Ms. Meyers smiled "Dave tells me Buddy got the best of you this week?"

I turned so she could see my swollen jaw "He was aiming for Curtis."

"I hope you got that checked. And look at Paul he is getting so big" She left to talk to them.

Dave came in around eleven and watched Brittany and Amelia; long enough for me to check on Jupiter who seemed to be hiding in a corner.

"Let's talk" I sat next to him.

"Oh I am fine, just staying completely clear of the girls."

"Ok, I am here if you need me."

By one Tiffany had sent herself into a panic; I tried to remind her that Sadie still had school today; but with Lynn teasing her it was useless. I had separated Brittany and Tiny at least fifty more times it seemed like I couldn't take my eyes off them for a nanosecond and Jupiter was still self separating.

"Hey Alex" Will came in as I was separating the girls again, Cater right beside him.

"Bless you save her, she for once isn't picking the fights" I handed her right to him.

"Are you sure that is my girlfriend?" Will asked, giving me an incredulous look.

Carter laughed "Tiny, not picking a fight hmm, slightly scary."

"Scary, odd, unnerving or not, it is not her starting the fights" I was losing patients.

"Well then, beautiful, let's go before Al comes to his senses" Will laughed taking Amelia's hand.

"He's not kidding that crazy jealous . . ." Tiny started.

"OUTSIDE, Amelia, tell him outside" I sighed.

Finally at what felt like it should have been midnight but was only three Sadie came running in "TIFFANY!" She ran into Tiffany's arms.

Genevieve laughed; Jupiter, Anthony, Paul and her were playing a board game.

"I missed you too" Tiffany held her close.

Without any one to torment Lynn sat watching TV and I had Dave bring Brittany back to her room so I could get a break, after her father came, even if it was only fifteen minutes.

At four I brought Genevieve to Dave, Lynn to time out, Anthony and Paul to Ana, and Tiffany to the infirmary. Then I went to wash the blood off my hands and arms.

Do I want to know?" Ana asked when I got back to her and the boys.

"The eye can bleed a lot, but let's go we have a busy afternoon." Lynn had thrown a book at Tiffany's eye as she was kissing Sadie good bye.

"Are my toys ok?" Anthony asked.

"Your toys are right where you left them" I buckled him in. "We have to go home and change, I need a shower . . ."

"Does Tiffany need an eye patch like a pirate?" Paul giggled.

"No" I laughed "Just a Band-aid; then dinner and off to the pool hall."

"Again?" Anthony asked.

"Yup it is what we do almost every Friday and Saturday nights."

He looked undone, but he would adjust.

*   *   *

Anthony and Paul sat at a booth sharing a banana split; Anthony had head phones on. Ana, Samantha, Debbie and one of their other friends, Madeline, were sitting with the boys gushing over a bridal magazine looking at dress styles. Uncle Marc was trying to show me how to set up the sound system wires, but I was off in space watching Lorenzo. He was in the back with Adam and Jr.; that was making me nervous.

"Alex focus, please, it may look easy but it isn't your Mama color coded it when she was fifteen, blue to orange, green to red, purple to yellow and black to white."

"Wow!"

"What? Alex, are you listening?" Uncle Marc sighed.

"Um yeah Mama set the wires up, why didn't you?"

"I didn't know how, C.J. and her did."

"Oh so . . ."

"Nice try no digging, go get your cousin, Christian Said he gets to play roadie after he was rude to customers last week.

"Um Uncle Marc I think you should look up" I gulped; Jr., Adam and Lorenzo were up on the pool table pole dancing with the pool cues.

"MARC RAMON WILLIAMS Jr." My uncle yelled louder than he could have spoke into microphone before jumping off the stage and running towards him. The whole room got quite; Adam, Jr., and Lorenzo took off running. Uncle Donavan caught Lorenzo by the ear because he made the mistake of running towards the bar. Mama caught Jr. and Adam. I gulped I almost felt for them as my uncles dragged them into the kitchen. Normal noise and movement returned and I went back to the sound system check I was supposed to be doing. I wasn't getting very far and was getting very frustrated very fast severely wishing I had paid attention.

"Would you like some help?" Mrs. Wittson's sister asked me standing near the edge of the stage.

"Um, hi, yes please if you understand these?" I asked hopeful.

"Wires? No, your mama yes."

"Would you tell me about her?"

"Other than she likes art and hates history and was a straight A college student, I can't, sorry. But I can get Kyle she made this mess for him."

"For Dr. Wittson" I laughed remembering the video I was showed of Mama as a kid."

"He had um . . . Issues is the best way to put it, good luck I will go get him."

"Thank-you Ma' . . ."

"Call me Kat, Alex, we are both adults, you can relax a little."

"Yes, Ms. Kat."

She shook her head and got Dr. Wittson's attention for me.

"Dr. Wittson?" I asked as we worked.

"Yes Alex?"

"Why did Mama . . ."

"Stop right there Alex, I won't disrespect her."

"I mean the wires . . ."

"Oh she was helping me study bio, it's been painted and faded over the years but if you look really close at the chipping paint you can see there were cell parts drawn and wrote on it. I had to match the word to the pictures. The weird colors she painted over it were so Dad didn't know I was having trouble in school, he just thought it was a C.J. and J.J. thing."

"Oh ok can you help me plug the main microphone in?"

"Well um" He laughed "let's see red to green and blue to um . . ." He scratched at the paints "Orange, yellow goes to mitochondria or purple and black to white because those are the actual wires never pained never drawn on." He unplugged them all "Hear you try."

I covered my ears as it caused a loud high pitched noise from the main microphone being too close to the one in his hand backing up that I had the colors matched correctly.

Dr. Wittson laughed and backed up "Sorry, sound test rookie." He apologized to the crowd.

I blushed.

We set all the microphones back on their proper stands.

"Picture what it sounded like in here until I learned to diagram the cell properly" Dr. Wittson laughed.

I laughed.

"I learned quickly to match the cell parts. And after I passed my test Jess painted over the drawings."

Lorenzo carried a guitar and my sticks on stage, muttering to himself.

"Your own fault" I said.

"It was just a little fun, now I have to spend all of tomorrow scrubbing wood floors" Lorenzo whined.

"Hush, child!" Uncle Christian growled "That is inappropriate behavior."

"I'm twelve; you know there are child labor laws."

"You aren't being paid; it's called community service, chores, or your life now. Whichever you wish to call it; get over it and do it silently."

"More like slavery" Lorenzo yelled.

I swallowed hard and tried to shoot a pleading look to Ana's dad, who was checking his keyboard and guitar, but he didn't look up. Uncle Christian grabbed Lorenzo by the ear and dragged him back to the kitchen.

"He's dumber . . ."

"Than we thought" Twins stood next to the stage.

"Yes, yes he is" I agreed "What can I do for you two?"

"Help . . ."

"With a . . ."

"Girl."

"One girl guys?"

"Yes, well . . ."

"No one for . . ."

"Each of us."

"Ok, so other than you creeps are beyond help; where are these girls?"
Christopher pointed to two girls playing pool.

"Have you tried talking to them?"

"We tried . . ."

"Once but . . ."

"I got nervous . . ."

"So we came . . ."

"To you . . ."

"Wait who got nervous?"

"ME!" Christian said severely offended.

"Sorry I was listening, just not looking" I sighed. "Can you to function separately?"

"Obviously . . ."

"But why . . ."

"Should we . . ."

"We are . . ."

"Awesome . . ."

"Right anyway, just go over there and let Christopher talk until Christian feels confident enough to join conversation."

"Ok . . ."

"We will . . ."

"Try thank . . ."

"You, Al . . ."

"Uh-huh, just guys maybe you should also not . . ." They were off "Talk like that" I sighed.

*   *   *

After three sets and helping in the bar I went back to check on Paul and Anthony. Lorenzo was lying on a cot in between them, looking positively miserable. I resisted the urge to laugh, Paul and Anthony were both sound asleep.

"Al is that you?" Adam called from the other side of the prep table "Can you get Uncle Mike the Co2 thing is leaking again."

"Yep or . . ." I walked over turned off the system tightened the lose bolt and turned it back on "Clean the mess before your father sees."

"Um thanks."

"Yep, just clean the mess I don't want to be here all night I am tired."

"Tell the slave driver he . . ." Lorenzo growled.

"I value my life, and you were out of line. You are not the first and won't be the last person to mouth off and end up on a cot or scrubbing something."

He swore at me, so I just walked away.

*   *   *

At home I went to the roof, Ana had chastised me for not going straight to bed, but I was too focused on other things. There had to be someone willing to tell me about Mama how was I suppose to be a good person, father, and husband if I didn't know how my parents did it; they were famous I couldn't go anywhere without my name alone being protection for someone being harassed for being homosexual or it being associated with music, or with my uncles for being hard working and honest. I started to get that over whelming feeling I got when I was younger and my parents still toured and the reporters would try to ask me things or take my picture. Grandma had told me about Mom up until she moved in with Mama. I went down stairs to find Uncle Danny hoping he would talk to me he seemed different than my other uncles less into the "we obey Marc" rule.

"Al, even if I didn't fear my older siblings' wrath; I am the wrong person to ask. I couldn't tell you what you don't already know. I will try but if this gets back to Marc it is back on your own head not mine."

"Why do you call her J.J.?"

"Nick name."

"What's the other 'J' for?"

"I don't know; I didn't meet her until she was already J.J."

"What was she like as a kid?"

"I don't know I am seven years younger than her we got pictures and photo copies of report cards I met her for the first time when I was four didn't see her again until she was sixteen."

"What was she like as a teen then?"

He ran a frustrated hand through his hair "Al, these really are questions for her; she visited Mom when she was forced to and that was far and few between. When I was eight Mom let Jesse and I take drum lessons from her and Marc, she also occasionally let us watch them play in the pool hall. She didn't talk much and had head phones on most of the time, she wore long sleeve shirts occasionally drenched in blood, or occasionally the blood was visible but I know she told you about her cutting."

"Did anyone say why she didn't talk, or why the head phones? Yeah the cutting I know all about."

"Nope, that was just her; and that is all there was to it. In case you missed it my brother isn't big on people asking questions. I saw Mike and C.J. more. When they did something completely wrong they were sent to Mom's for varying lengths of time."

"So Mama behaved?"

"Or just didn't get caught" He shrugged "Have you tried talking to her?"

"Kind of, she just tells me that her past doesn't matter. Did you know my mom back then too?"

"Sort of she would talk to me. She was as mouthy as Colt and as quiet as Nick. You are your father, quiet, smart, tall, protective, but you have your mother's mental stability, allergies and patients."

I frowned "Are you saying she is crazy?"

"No neither are you, I mean the anxiety, now my sister on the other hand there have been bets on that behind Marc's back starting with your father."

"Why" I laughed.

"You live with her . . ."

"Well um . . . ok yeah, all those charts."

"Is there more or can I go to bed?"

"Do you know anyone who could tell me that isn't terrified of Uncle Marc?"

"Your mother when she is ready too" Uncle Christian growled from behind me.

I gulped.

"Andare a letto, Alexander (Go to bed, Alexander).

"Yes, sir" I gulped harder.

"Ora!"

"Yes, sir."

"Dan, that was not polite to your sister, and if Marc finds out you will be at fault" Uncle Christian confronted Uncle Danny

"I am not worried; I know nothing of what he was looking for and mostly it was of Tina he asked and of his father not my sister" Uncle Danny went to bed.

"Ok"

CHAPTER 11

WEEKEND

"Get up" Uncle Christian said "Karate."

I had forgot to set the alarm "Sorry."

"No sorry, just get up."

I shook Ana and dressed quickly I would shower after karate.

"Jess" Eric shook his head "What did you do to Alex, he looks awful."

"Not me" Mama laughed "He was up harassing Danny last night."

"No digging" Uncle Marc growled at me as he dropped Adam and Jr. off.

"No Marc, my big dumb rock caught him asking of himself" Mama laughed.

I sighed audibly someone had covered for me.

Uncle Marc looked at me "Your Mama will . . ."

"Talk when she is ready" I groan and went to the changing room.

"Mmm" Uncle Marc grumbled.

"Marc, let up, Al is fine or J.J. would say something" Mom stared him down "I think he is just worried about being a good parent."

"He need not worry" Uncle Marc said with so much surety it was startling "See you later."

"If I didn't know how genetics worked . . ." Mom shook her head.

Eric laughed "Or you could just tell your extremely stubborn wife the world won't end if her son knows she isn't and never was perfect."

"I have but she's . . . ."

"Stubborn, impulsive . . ."

"Impossible!"

Eric just laughed and shook his head.

*　　　*　　　*

After karate we took care of the horses, and then I showered. I nearly scrubbed my skin off. Ana took the boys outside to play and I had practice.

"Heart breaker . . . I don't need to practice this" Uncle Chris objected, breaking the song.

"C.J" Uncle Marc sighed "You . . ."

"Alex plays just fine and after this long I bet even Don could play it."

Uncle Don stuck his head out of his room "Don does not play and or sing music, Don enjoys your music."

Uncle Christian laughed and mouthed to me "Dying fish sing better."

I choked trying not to laugh.

"Issues little boy" My Uncle glared at me.

"No sir, Uncle Donavan, just reading tonight's play list, sir."

"Right" He shook his head at my bad lying "Piccolo fratello (little brother) I don't sing like a dead fish for they sing far better than I ever could."

I laughed unable not to; he said it with such a serious face.

"Fine, fine well you pick one" Uncle Marc groaned at Uncle Chris.

"I am rusty on No Greater Love." Dr. Wittson offered.

We played No greater love and four other songs before dinner. We made it through dinner without any one soaping Lorenzo's mouth, in fact despite the day before Lorenzo was getting slowly day by day less mouthy or well at least less vulgar. Dinner was good it was steak and potatoes; mom's favorite. I was nervous about playing tonight I had never played No Greater Love before today; I had heard it plenty of times but never played it.

"Al" Miss Nikki stopped me outside as I was reloading my drums into the back of Uncle Marc's truck "Your godfather."

"I am sorry?"

"It is the answer Dan couldn't give you last night."

"My godfather" I hadn't even thought of that "Thank-you."

"Don't thank me, Danny paid me to, Christian scares him more than Marc.

I laughed "Uncle Christian is very scary at three am but you won't talk to me?"

"Nope, can't imagine A.J. going against her either, he is her best . . ."

"I meant Uncle Chris, Ma'am."

"Oh sorry let me guess why he won't marry . . ."

"Why does he hate 'Heart Breaker'?"

"I told you it is about him, but have you tried asking him?"

"Would he actually answer me?"

"I bet he would. Are you alright you look green."

"Nerves, I don't know how Mama did it; she herself said she hated crowds."

"You asking?"

"Nope, it was rhetorical."

"Well, even if you are I will answer that one, head phones and your father."

"My father?"

"He had a unique gift of scaring people same as his brothers do."

"Oh" I said it wasn't the most intelligent response but it is what I said.

*　　*　　*

"Phone was shut off yesterday and the cable it's out too and I spent my last dollar fifty on a rose for you now we are sitting here eating breakfast and I'm reading the classifieds because . . .

artist aint a real job yeah that's what they said bills don't pay themselves and you can't live on love but oh baby if we could we'd be the richest people in this town because baby I'm still in love with you but artist aint a real job and love don't pay the bills.

I look up over my coco cup he's standing on a chair stretching for his orange juice I pick him up and hand him his cup he points at your picture and he smiles "mom that's mommy" with a deep breath I tell him yeah and look into his deep green eyes there just like yours you know I take a deep sigh and go back to the classifieds because . . .

artist aint a real job yeah that's what they said bills don't pay themselves and you can't live on love but oh baby if we could we'd be the richest people in this town because baby I'm still in love with you but artist aint a real job and love don't pay the bills.

I look at my list of thing to do today and smile up at him he's playing with the train he got last year for Christmas and boy he's getting big I can't believe he's already three has it really been that long I clear off the table story hour starts in five so I drive him there yeah I finally got my license no it didn't take me long once I set my mind to it he says I love you mom as I drop him off and head up to the computers still looking for a job . . .

artist aint a real job yeah that's what they said bills don't pay themselves and you can't live on love but oh baby if we could we'd be the richest people in this town because baby I'm still in love with you but artist aint a real job and love don't pay the bills.

I take him up to see your grave and give you the rose we bought, the letter I wrote, and the picture he drew maybe when he's older I'll explain to him what happened and how it was true love and why he writes and reads like you and draws and sings like me heaven help my ear he likes to sing and why he looks like you and who his daddy is but for now I need a job because . . .

artist aint a real job yeah that's what they said bills don't pay themselves and you can't live on love but oh baby if we could we'd be the richest people in this town because baby I'm still in love with you but artist aint a real job and love don't pay the bills."

Paul was in my arms, trying to help me play and Anthony was playing pool with the twins when Mom finished singing No Greater Love. Lorenzo was sitting at the bar he wasn't allowed to leave Uncle Don's sight. I looked for Ana and found the one person I had been avoiding for two weeks. When the set ended I flew off stage and into the kitchen.

"Hiding from someone?" Aunt Amy asked.

"Nope, thinking" I breathed hard.

"Really?" Mama frowned coming in behind me "I just spoke to Charlie, march your butt right back out there and speak to him."

"Yes Ma'am."

Aunt Amy laughed "He is Tina too not just Colt."

"MMM, tell me about it" Mama shook her head.

"He ok?"

"Yep, just stubborn."

*   *   *

"Part of being a famous person's son is everyone knows where you are and when you are there. You play well, but there is a lot of pressure in the lime light" Charlie was standing outside the kitchen door.

"Less now that I am out of school" I scowled I worked very hard at ignoring all the recognition I got for who my parents were, unless it got me somewhere with a child like Lynn that fist day.

"Even though you are now playing with the band?"

"Still less."

"I bet you know why I am here."

"I would hope it was to enjoy the music and the food, but I am not that foolish, I skipped again."

"Oh I enjoy the music and ken makes the best curly fries in town but you are accurate I am here to speak to you."

"Um . . . how is next Wednes . . ."

"Nope I am here to talk to you now until your next set."

I sighed audibly and looked around frustrated.

"Sit and listen," Ana scowled on her way in to the kitchen.

"I was looking for a quiet booth" I objected.

Charlie laughed "She loves you."

"She *is* my fiancé, as you pointed out I can't escape the media attention from my mothers' name, you should know that, four different papers had me pictured buying the ring I am surprised she didn't know" If my mothers had heard me I would have been in trouble for being so rude but I was tired and miserable today and just wanted to get my work done as fast as possible so I could get some sleep. I led him to the quietest corner I could find.

He ignored my snide remarks "How have you been?"

"I am fine the weeks went by fast."

"How did your hearing go?"

"Good he is home permanently when he is level four."

"Does this bother you?"

"A little but not a lot he is a level three now and I only want what is best for him."

"And the crying?"

"Better, it is mostly now when I am past thirty-six hours of no sleep."

"Thirty-six hours of no sleep, wow I would cry too."

"Nah, it is the seventy-two the hurts."

"No wonder your family worries about you so much, have you considered sleep aids?"

"No, I refuse chemicals except the very necessary in my body."

"Ok, can I ask you something?"

I stared blankly at him.

"Are you opposed to counseling?"

"No, I am just truly this busy, I have two jobs, two sons, and my last semester of online college."

"Ok, what if I told you I have already spoke to Dave, and I can meet you on Wednesday mornings, would that help?"

I nodded "But I am busy then too."

"I mean at the center."

"Um ok, guess that would help."

"Good" He smiled "Go tell your mama I would like to speak to her about a train book my grandson is completely enamored with."

I laughed "Yes sir." On my way to find Mama I saw fans crowding my uncle Chris, Mom said he loved all the attention. Three girls ran up to me giggling waving pen and paper; they couldn't have been more than thirteen or fourteen.

"You're the new drummer in M2CJ right?" One squealed.

I thought my ears were going to exploded "Um yeah, I am Alex."

"Will you sign theses?"

"How tall are you?"

"Are you single?"

"How old are you?"

"Um . . . I took the pen and signed each paper "I am seven feet tall, I have brown hair brown eyes and a fiancé, and um I am almost twenty-two."

They squealed really loudly in my ears and ran off in to the crowd.

"Al, you alright?" Ana's dad asked me.

"Huh? Oh yeah I am fine, just looking for Mama and became unexpectedly deaf for the evening, preteens to be exact" I laughed.

"Oh, they squeal the worst" He said knowingly "Jess and Kyle use to where the sound blocking head phones through the crowds, it hurt their ears so badly."

"Do you know where Mama is?"

"I distinctly remember her and Tina dancing through the kitchen, to piss off my sister."

I laughed my mothers took pride in aggravating my aunt Kate. "Dancing near the prep table again?"

"You know it."

I laughed harder "Thank you sir, see you on stage." I found Mama by the kitchen door having a 'chat' with Christian, so I waited until she was done reprimanding him for whatever insane thing he or Christopher had done this time; then I went to bus for the last fifteen minutes before I had to be on stage again.

Half way through the third set Uncle Marc read from the request can "Can you PLEASE play something that didn't have a number one spot on the radio, you big jerk?" Uncle Marc laughed "What song Danny?" He yelled a crossed to the bar where Uncle Danny was helping Uncle Donavan.

"Something other than lost soul, blinded, and heart breaker, *PLEASE.*" Uncle Danny yelled back.

"How about Cool Kid?" Someone in the crowd yelled.

Uncle Marc looked at me.

"I know it" I gulped hoping I knew what song they picked better than just knowing the name "Oh look I have the tabs".

"We normally end with Cool Kid so how about we play Push, it got no radio play by bands choice."

"Ouch that's old" Mr. Wittson laughed, he looked like he was trying to remember it.

Uncle Marc counted off and I had to scramble to find the right tabs because I had only heard the song once in practice.

Mom sang "You push and you push and you push but I don't go nowhere, you been pushing so long and pushing so hard I bet you don't even remember why you are trying to push me away."

I struggled a little at first but caught up relatively fast and by the chorus I was able to tell that this was a product of someone fighting.

"So why don't you just give up, why don't you just let it be let you love me. I am not made of straw I will not blow away I am not made of wood I will not rot and break away and although I am not stone I am just as strong have a little faith in me when I say I am here to stay, yours for keeps you can trust me.

Day in and day out it's the same old fight, you push and I push right back it's like you haven't even noticed that this won't get you very far I see it in your eyes it is tiring you more than me.

So why don't you just give up, why don't you just let it be let you love me. I am not made of straw I will not blow away I am not made of wood I will not rot and break away and although I am not stone I am just as strong have a little faith in me when I say I am here to stay, yours for keeps you can trust me.

Can't you see she's not me? I won't break your heart or tear you a part. Look me in the eyes and tell me you deny your love for me."

Uncle Chris sang the bridge it gave it an odd twist "You push and you push and you push some more, I bet you don't even know or care why or what your pushing for anymore. Open your eyes and hear me out."

Mom went back to singing "So why don't you just give up, why don't you just let it be let you love me. I am not made of straw I will not blow away I am not made of wood I will not rot and break away and although I am not stone I am just as strong have a little faith in me when I say I am here to stay, yours for keeps you can trust me.

Don't put me on a pedestal, don't look at me with hurt and hate I am not the bad guy here. Truth be told you always have been your own worst enemy. Take a step back and look at me before you push away think before you speak. Time is changing skin deep beauty it is fleeting my patients it is wearing thin. You say you care you say you want me here's your chance give it up let it be let me love you

So why don't you just give up, why don't you just let it be let you love me. I am not made of straw I will not blow away I am not made of wood I will not rot and break away and although I am not stone I am just as strong have a little faith in me when I say I am here to stay, yours for keeps you can trust me."

*　　　*　　　*

"Up" Paul demanded.

"What?" I yawned.

"Up" He demanded again "*My* horse is waiting on me!"

"Ooh Not with that attitude" Ana woke up faster and smoother than I ever could "March your little tail down those stairs to breakfast. It is seven thirty your horse isn't even awake yet."

"Seven thirty" I groaned grabbing clean clothes for my shower.

When I came out of the shower Anthony was sitting between Mama and Uncle Chris eating pancakes no one else was up.

"Morning Mama" I greeted her "Can I talk to A.J. today?"

"Sure" She looked at me lost "I will call him."

"Dad, Paul woke me"? Anthony yawned.

"Sorry he is still learning that only he likes getting up this early" I yawned "Paul we don't wake Anthony just because he is there, he will be more willing to play with you if you let him wake up on his own" I picked Paul up to sit him in his booster seat.

"Yes I do!" He snapped kicking at me "You can't tell me what to do!"

"Time out Paul" I sat him in the corner.

"Bad choice Paul, it is not even eight thirty and you have lost two stars" Ana marked his chart. We had started it Wednesday Mama said it would take about two weeks.

He screeched at Ana "I HATE YOU!"

"That's nice I love you too" Ana had to go out of the room to avoid arguing with him.

Anthony looked terrified every time we put Paul in time out, he kept watching Ana like she was going to lash out and start beating them. Paul seemed to think it was funny to push my patience.

"Paul, you are going to be dinning on soap if you don't quit screeching no at me" I sighed, he was in time out for the fifth time before lunch.

"Again Paul" Mama frowned. "Al, A.J. will be here at one."

"Thanks Mama" I looked up from Paul's grill cheese and ham.

112

"You're welcome" She looked at Paul's lunch.

"It is all he eats."

"It's ok Al, you went through a period where all you ate was celery, raisins, and peanut butter; for about a year and a half. I thought there was something wrong with you I was so panicked I had all your grandparents check you and several different doctors, I thought you had some weird disease" Mom laughed.

"Paul, Anthony lunch."

"Grill cheese again?" Anthony crinkled his nose.

"No, sorry here, I swapped the plates "Yours is the steamed veggie bowl see."

Paul looked at Anthony's bowl and stole a carrot.

"Wouldn't do that kiddo, he may get mad and stab your hand one day" Uncle Chris joked.

"C.J.!" Mom scolded "Don't tell them things like that."

I rolled my eyes "Here Paul" I put a few carrots on his plate and one back on Anthony's.

While Paul napped Ana took Anthony with her to her father's and I met with my godfather in the studio, thankfully Uncle Donavan was upstairs.

"What's up Alex? I doubt you are calling me to see if you can play laser tag with my sons and I know you don't need me to baby sit you" My godfather sat on my drum stool so I hopped up on the washer.

I blushed "Um no, I have some questions, about . . . about Mama."

"Mmhmm, I won't answer if you knowing it will upset her and I think it would be nice if you waited for her, but I think we both may die before she talks."

"What's the second "J" in J.J. for?" I smiled.

"Really, yeah, no, next" He shook his head "I am not an all knowing genie, her and I didn't even go to the same school."

I laughed; he looked so confused "Why the constant head phones?"

"Same as you, music is soothing."

"Uncle Danny said she had them . . ."

"Next!"

"Ok, I get it. Why didn't she live with grandma?"

"I don't know?"

"What do you know?" I laughed.

"That you're a smart ass like your mother, and I know she is my best friend" He laughed.

"Dave said she use to steal you?"

"Steal is a harsh word, liberate is more accurate it was my weekend, an orphan in state custody with a self injury problem back then you were automatically labeled and placed there until you were eighteen."

"How did you meet Mama?"

"Community service."

"You or . . ."

"Both."

"Why did she have community service?"

"I don't know" He laughed "She never told me and to me it didn't matter."

"Oh, what was she like?"

He sighed "To me she was nice, she didn't speak a lot and when she did it wasn't always clear what she said or what she was trying to say. Learning disabilities I suspect don't know; she is so fiercely self motivating that I bet even a psychologist wouldn't know."

"The million and ten calendar charts?"

"I thought that was Christian, that's J.J hmm next."

I laughed "Maybe it is Uncle Christian and Mama just writes them for him."

Uncle Christian came in from outside "Hello A.J."

"Hey Christian how are you?" A.J. greeted him and gave me an "I am sorry look".

"I am good, did your Godson tell you his son will be home permanently soon?"

"J.J. did a week ago."

Uncle Christian sat with his Guitar on the dryer "So what were you two talking about that everyone is up stairs?"

I suppressed a groan.

"They were up there to begin with; we were talking about my community service." A.J. covered. Points to my uncle Danny, A.J. wasn't afraid of Uncle Marc or Uncle Christian.

Uncle Christian laughed "Which time? The library or . . ."

"I was about to tell him about the park."

"Well don't let me stop you."

"As I was saying, Al, I had just turned fifteen and had got caught stealing diapers for Tyler . . ."

"You weren't always at C.H.T.D.C.?" I asked.

"Nope, I was with a foster family until I was sixteen. Anyway the first community service it was for the fist fight I got in with Ana's mom over the diapers I stole from her fathers' store. They had us cleaning the park it was me two other guys and a girl" He winked at me. "The guys stood talking, the girl on the other hand did not she scrubbed at the spray paint we were scrubbing off a bench like it was a personal offense. So I tried to speak to her; that went as well as my fist fight with Nalanie had. I asked her name and when I matched the name to her older brother she decked me, rather hard I might add, broke my jaw."

Uncle Christian shook his head "As I recall Jason said that young lady decidedly broke your nose and cheek bone that day too."

"Ow" I raised an eyebrow, I had heard Uncle Christian mention his and A.J.'s friend, Jason, from high school before "Why?"

"Because I asked her about herself" A.J. sighed "I asked if she had a boyfriend and she hit my noses square on, told me that she had a . . . girlfriend." I knew what he meant I had heard Mama at pride events and other things say she had a Tina not a wife or a girlfriend, or a life partner like some people said. "I asked her what she liked to do in her spare time and she broke my cheek bone and told me it was none of my damn business, she finally stopped hitting me when I stopped asking about her and started talking about me."

"I distinctly remember Jason calling me to come get you because you made a fatal mistake" Uncle Christian said.

"I asked her why she was bleeding after our lunch break." My Godfather shook his head "Only asked her something like that once. She dove at me, knocked me to the ground slamming my head into a rock until I was unconscious."

*　　　*　　　*

I didn't get any more information out of my godfather thanks to my uncle but I caught the message loud and clear: Mama didn't like to discuss certain things. After Paul and Anthony went to bed I sat on the roof staring into space. The second "J" in Mama's nick name bothered me almost more than the violent person A.J, had depicted.

Mom sat down near me "Ok, what's up three hours you have been out here with no coat; you're going to get sick."

"Mama was violent?"

Mom sighed "Alex, you have cut before, you work in a self injury wing of a detention center, she has told you herself before she was not a very approachable person."

"That's not . . ."

"You my love need some patients, your Mama is a very stubborn woman and she loves you boys with her whole heart, soul, and being. She isn't trying to drive you crazy, she just feels that her past is just that her past and it needs to stay in the past" Mom wrapped her arms around me "Is this about Paul and Anthony?"

"No, I just, I don't know."

"I heard you blew Charlie off two weeks in a row."

"Yeah" I blushed "I won't do that again I don't even know why I blew him off other than I felt weak."

Mom laughed "Even if you weren't Alexander Williams he would have still found you he's good like that. But what were you thinking trying to hide? But you are Alexander Joseph Williams, you should know

116

by now you can't hide much of anything if you aren't recognized by your name for the books, music, and work in the gay pride community your fiancé's family owns half this town. How do you think we caught Christian and Christopher skipping back in September, your Uncle Tim saw them sneaking in to the theater, there were three pictures and you, Henry and Davie saw them sneaking back out. Your mama has eight brothers, six sister-in-laws, one brother-in-law and parents. I have two brothers, one sister-in-law and my mom. Ana has a brother, her father and her father has a sister and two brothers with wives. That does not include your or her cousins. All of us are active in the community with friends; Adam once told your uncle that it was like farting in a fish bowl and then the media saw you."

I shuddered "Please don't remind me I work very hard at ignoring the . . . hey why don't we have your maiden name?"

Mom laughed "Because I took her name so of course your last name is Williams, Goober I think you need more sleep at night."

"Did you ever tour with Mama?"

"No."

"Even before we were born"

"No I never went with them; the crowds at the pool hall were almost too much for me, on tour your mama and C.J. sang"

"Did they stop touring because of us?"

"No they stopped touring because your uncle could no longer back flip off stage."

"Uncle Chris can still flip."

"Stubborn, prideful, Neanderthal Marc cannot, with his back" Mom laughed.

"Oh" I laughed too. "Did you know Dr. Wittson had trouble in biology?"

"Learned the sound system I see" She hugged tighter "Look at you my big baby all grown up and getting married."

"UHG!"

"What?" She laughed "Have you changed your mind?"

"No it's just a lot of hurry up and wait."

"You sound like your daddy" Mama sat down on my other side.

"He sounds like you" Mom teased her.

"He is right thought" Mama smiled, I saw a glint of the twins' evil in her eyes.

"You both hush it will be worth it and you *both* know it will" Mom laughed.

"I know I am just having location indecision trying to find a beach."

"I know a private one" Mom offered "Nalanie grew up on it."

"Does someone live there now?" I asked.

"No the house was torn down about seven years ago but the beach is still there I can make some calls tomorrow morning for you. But right now it's late you might want to go to sleep you have work in the morning."

"Thank you Mama."

CHAPTER 12

LONG WEEK

Monday started with a bang and I don't mean Anthony's temper tantrum over going back or Brittany and Tiny fighting. I mean an actual bang sound from the A-hall, and lots of smoke. Somehow one of the kids had gotten some cherry bombs and smoke bombs; it caused three hours of Chaos.

"If your Mama weren't a grown woman; I would say this was her handy work" Dave laughed as another smoke bomb went off close to us.

"She is helping Mom get ready for Thursday, but did you check around for my brothers?" I grabbed a confused looking child sending him to the café.

"Actually I did; they are in school."

I laughed "Are you sure those beasts weren't happy with the hearing verdict."

"I think it's that seventeen year the court brought in last night for meth."

"Lovely" I rolled my eyes.

We were following the bangs and smoke but they were not all in the same hall or going off in neat rows and the smoke was making it hard. Finally after three hours of it Ana got irritated as she was trying to work, never a good idea to interrupt Ana when she was busy. Ana caught the girl and brought her by her ear straight to Rodger."

Dave was impressed "Her Mama would be proud."

I nodded my memories of her mom were good but she had that air to her, you did not disrespect her in anyway. After the morning mess nothing on Monday at work fazed me.

At home Paul was on a tear, having a full fledged tantrum in time out. I apologized to my parents again, but they swore up and down he was fine and it was no problem; but according to his chart he hadn't been fine at all better than Sunday but still nowhere near fine.

Tuesday was long I had Amelia and Brittany. Dave swore it was because I was good at my job. I was almost a hundred percent positive it was because no one else would take Brittany and Amelia was my responsibility. With or without Brittany, Tiny only listened to Dave or I and Tuesdays Dave always had all day meetings and or paper work this week it was meetings. I thought it would be easy and they would both end in time out or their rooms right away, but they didn't. The girls picked at, poked at and teased each other all day long never doing anything cruel enough to end up in time out. By five I was so completely annoyed and irritated that I spent an hour in the time out room myself crying and rocking fighting the urge to cut and the flood of flash backs/ withdrawals.

At home Paul had, had a relatively good day, but Lorenzo on the other hand had not causing me to walk into a yelling match between him and Uncle Christian.

Paul was running around in his pajamas completely unphased "Hi Daddy."

I picked him up and edged carefully in to his room as to avoid crossfire of the argument. Any adult would be crazy to willingly get into the middle of a fight like that.

"Orenzo hits people" Paul smiled at me proudly.

"I can hear that how about you pick your books and we will read six instead of four tonight."

"I has to pick up ants firsts" He ran back to the living room.

I peeked out his bedroom door and looked towards Mama's room where Uncle Danny was trying to get my attention to get me to go to him. I snuck down the hall "What happened?" I asked Mom when I was safe in her room.

"His mouth" Uncle Chris sighed.

"He can hear that C.J." Mom frowned "We can all hear that. The school called he was caught fist fighting with someone, and when your uncle asked what happened at school he chose to run his mouth instead of telling us what happened. The school said he did not start it."

"Letto ora (bed now)!" Uncle Christian yelled loud enough to be heard in Mom and Mama's room clearly "And you are grounded."

"Didn't he just . . ." Ana came in and stopped mid sentence.

"Where's Al?" Uncle Christian asked as nicely as he could despite his mood.

"I am in here with Mom" I quickly answered.

"Your Mama is out here with me" The tone in his voice said you will get out here too now.

"She is crazy" I whispered to Uncle Danny on my way to the kitchen. I greeted Mama and didn't get to close to my still fuming uncle.

"He is all bark and no bite" Mama laughed watching me cautiously edge around Uncle Christian. "Anyway I called the town and then the people whom currently own the beach and you have one reserved private beach for your wedding on July fourth."

"Thanks Mama."

"I will be back, if he even breaths out of line call me" Uncle Christian slammed out the back door.

"That doesn't scare you?" I looked at her.

She stared back at me blankly.

*   *   *

Wednesday morning ten a.m. I met Charlie at security more like Dave tied me to the security gate until Charlie got there; I smiled slightly trying not to groan "Morning."

"Morning, where are we going to talk?"

"Time out room, I have time share stock in there."

He laughed at the joke but I was serious. I had once offered to pay day rental for the room after a long week of fighting with Ana right after graduation.

"You look rattled today" He said.

"It is Wednesday, Sundays are better."

"Ok then, let's talk about triggers today."

I stared at him blankly,

"For cutting . . ."

I started at him blankly "I know what you meant."

"Well then list them."

I sighed "Crowds, media stress, my temper."

"Ok let's talk about crowds, you walk through the pool hall and play on stage."

"I am almost twenty-two I have coping skills also that isn't my biggest trigger it is just the one I choose to share with the kids here."

"It never affects you anymore?"

"I didn't say that I said it is not my largest trigger" I laid back on the soft mattress and closed my eyes trying to focus on my temper control.

"I could see how you would like it in here; a room full of beds" He laughed. "What is your most life affecting trigger?"

"The back lash from the media and press, there is no privacy I find it over whelming and very stressful."

"I don't see any of that here?"

"Dave put a stop to it when I first started here; also there isn't any at the house because my uncles offered to cram a camera up somewhere unpleasant. Before I was born my Uncles had to have restraining orders placed, and since Mama and Uncle Chris stopped touring the amount has gone down to just around the pool hall, when there is a book tour coming up for a new book, or when . . .

"Like this?" He pulled out a news paper one of the four that covered me buying Ana's ring.

I groaned "I told you it was a miracle that she didn't already know. But yes exactly like that slow local news days and large gay pride segments. Like I said it is much better now that I am older and out of high school."

"I can image it is easier, so what happens with the media pressure?"

"Crippling panic attacks."

"Have you considered anxiety meds?"

I glared at him.

"Right chemicals, just a suggestion; so how do you cope with your panic now?"

"Deep breaths and yoga" I rolled my eyes.

"Are you sure you don't have issues with consoling?"

"Nope, just had a moment, sorry."

"No it's ok I am guessing working here your moments are needed."

"Fighting teen girls."

He laughed "Understood."

"We have a punching bag I take it out on, so when I feel caged, trapped, over whelmed I do that or I go up to the roof to meditate, I also listen to music and play my drums."

"Did adopting the boys change that?"

"Nope, actually it improved it gave me an extra positive outlet because no matter how bad my day a hug from them even hearing or seeing them and Ana makes the world brighter and better, it is like they make everything feel right, like I am invincible and can do anything and everything."

*　　　*　　　*

At home we were celebrating Mom's book tour with a special dinner and family time as Mom was leaving first thing in the morning. Ana and I had gotten her earrings to match the blouse that Kenny and the twins had bought her. Paul's chart was improving and Lorenzo was silent. Uncle Chris was last minute packing and giving a million directions to someone on the other end of the phone.

I was so tired that after I put Paul to bed I went to bed. My mind was racing and it took a while but once I was asleep with Ana in my arms I slept soundly, no dreams just deep solid sleep.

Thursday was boring Dave had me filing, he said it was so I could have extra one on one with Anthony once he was done with his school work and counseling; I think he was just afraid of me fully awake. At home everything was peaceful and I was able to do home work and then I slept soundly again.

My sleeping well should have been a sign of bad things to come, thankfully it wasn't work though. Work went like every other Friday fighting and all, but nothing out of the ordinary for a Friday. Anthony, Paul and I signed out Anthony and met Ana at the car. It was even calm at home. Then Mama told the boys that they did not have to go to the pool hall if they did not want too. Davie, whom never went unless he had to or had a date, had asked on Wednesday if he could have the boys over night for quality time. After dinner Ana helped them pack an overnight bag and walked them a crossed the drive way while I loaded my drums in to the back of a van.

Around ten two officers came in that wasn't odd; good music, good food, pool, darts, bar, and routine checks for different things. But the officers came straight over to me.

"This your I.D., sir?" The officer I didn't recognize asked showing me my driver's license; the name on his badge said Greene. I had never seen him and with the beasts for brothers I had met a lot of cops.

"Yes, thank you very much" I took it "I have been looking everywhere for it, Ana had to drive today. How are you Officer Demin? I think Mrs. Wittson is in the kitchen with Mama."

JUST ALEX

"I am fine Alex, but I am not here to see my daughter, I think you should grab your Mama and come with us your brother had your license."

"Uh-oh" I breathed there was only one brother that would need my license. Kenny and the twins had licenses of their own and we had dropped Nick off at his girlfriends.

Someone had alerted Mama before I could "Officers, can I help you; is Alex in trouble."

"Not unless he gave his brother his license to drink and drive" The new guy said.

"HE WHAT!" Mama shrieked.

"J.J, really, take it outside" Mr. Wittson said before seeing the cops, "Oh sorry officers."

"It's fine Ken; come on Jess, Ken is right let's go outside" Officer Demin suggested.

"Gladly my youngest is going to wish his mother was not on book tour" Mama muttered all the way out the door.

Sitting in the back of the cruiser looking seven steps past miserable were Lorenzo, Colt and Colts friend Jeffery.

"How did they get passed the clerk?" Mama looked at them and then me. "Not one of them is seven feet tall nor do they have Al's hair."

"They took that one's" Officer Demin indicated Jeffery with his chin "Parent's car over to Eighteenth and Simon, to the package store out there, they claim they weren't carded, but we are investigating that, two of our undercovers out there who caught them said to tell Al, he would see him next Friday."

"Tell Will and Cart I say hi" I said curiously.

"March" Mama growled at Lorenzo and Colt as they were let out of the car. "Lorenzo dishes, Colt find Adam or Jr. and have one of them teach you how to bus tables."

"Child labor laws . . ." Lorenzo started to argue.

"Move; you're lucky that it is me out here and not Donavan!"

Officer Demin laughed "Crystalline said that he was giving you all a lot of trouble. Don't worry they don't have court dates or anything I just gave them warnings. Your boy was positive I should keep him."

Mama shook her head "I am going to have the cleanest house in town."

I tried not to laugh.

"Are you sure you or Alex didn't know they had the license?" The new cop asked.

"Yeah I am sure, I just told you I have been looking everywhere for it! I have work to do" I stormed back inside.

Mama sighed "That would be why Colt wanted you to keep him. Al tore apart the house in front of those two and neither one said anything."

Officer Demin laughed "You should probably save them from Al then, we have to get that one to his parents."

*   *   *

"What the hell were you thinking!" I yelled at them "Drinking and Driving not to mention stealing my license."

"I wasn't drinking" Colt whimpered "I was the designated driver."

"Jeff took most of it" Lorenzo complained throwing pots in the sink. "I only got three sips and it was bourbon too."

"Non si dovrebbero avere avuto qualsiasi (You shouldn't have had any)! You are no longer grounded for two weeks you are now grounded until you are twenty-five. And Colt your honesty although always appreciated does not excuse the fact that you did steal your brother's license, you were driving unlicensed, or that not once did you say hey this is not a good idea or I am not joining in" Uncle Christian shook his head.

"My license! Why my license? You know if there had been an inspection at work I would have been screwed!" I started to go off again.

"Dave would have saved you" Colt mumbled to his feet.

"No, he couldn't have, not from that!"

"We look like you not Kenny and the things, it had to be yours" Lorenzo shrugged.

It took all I had not to dive at him

"If you didn't want it taken you shouldn't have left it on the table" Lorenzo rolled his eyes.

Colt swore at Lorenzo and they dived for each other. I grabbed Colt, Uncle Christian just let Lorenzo hit the floor.

"Siete fatto (done)!" Uncle Don Picked Lorenzo up off the floor "Lorenzo this kitchen will be spotless by one."

"Slav . . ." Soap was placed in Lorenzo's mouth.

"Without complaint Lorenzo. Piccolo fratello please take our nephew to Il vostro piccolo (Your little one) and Alex go back to work."

"I am working" I showed him the potato slicer and the potato.

CHAPTER 13

27, 28

After karate I called Will and Carter to personally thank them; they reassured me it was nothing and they would see me Friday. Colt was scrubbing the bathroom and Lorenzo the kitchen. Ana was playing chutes and ladders with Anthony and I had taken Paul to the horse stables with me and Uncle Christian. Mama was not letting Colt out of Uncle Donavan's sight.

"How was your week, Al?" Mama asked.

"Busy and long, Wednesday was the worst."

"I heard, Ana said it was an escape attempt."

"It was a mess, that's for sure, cherry and smoke bombs everywhere."

"Did anyone escape?"

"No."

"Then they didn't do it right" Mama said I saw the twins evil glint in her eyes again.

I laughed "Dave said that if you weren't grown he would have been looking for you as it was he called the school to make sure the twins were in class."

Mama laughed "If it were me it wouldn't have taken three hours"

"A.J. told me when I started there that you use to use the twins' father as a distraction."

"Yes I did, Jake was a sweet guy, crazy oh so crazy, but very sweet. He would do anything for beef jerky."

I laughed "Was he in there for cutting?"

"Nope, I don't know all the details but he was there just to have a roof over his head he actually went to the public school every day with your uncle Mike they are the same age. And you know Dave; he couldn't handle the thought of a kid being homeless. He put him in with A.J. and would have him up and out to a bus stop for school."

"Like Mohawk?"

"Yes like Sam, except Jake had no addictions."

I put Paul on the pony circle with Lizzy and Uncle Christian while Mama and I went riding. She rode fast hugging Emmy's neck like she forgot she had saddle and reigns. I rode fast too, but I sat up right using the reigns. It was gorgeous on the trails with the snow and ice encasing everything.

"You ok back there?" Mama called.

"Enjoying the ride" I laughed "You know Mama, they have reigns."

Mama laughed hugging tighter to Emmy "So I have been told."

After we were done at the stables Mama took Nick to the library and I took Anthony sledding. While Paul napped Ana did school work. The twins and Kenny were working and Uncle Donavan had Colt and Lorenzo cleaning everything in sight, still. We had pasta and sauce; Mama had taken Kenny out to dinner. I kind of almost felt sorry for Colt his one on one time with Mama would not be overly pleasant; no matter what he chose to do the conversation would be about proper choices and peer pressure. The twins were always getting brought home by the cops most of the time it was Officer Demin just giving them a ride home or dumb things like flashing cheerleaders. The worst for them would have either been the time Christopher had broken some ones nose or the time Christian had set fire crackers off inside the school.

We met Mama at the pool hall Lorenzo and Colt were scrubbing the pool hall. Kenny had picked up Juliet and they were at a booth. The twins were playing pool and Nick had my boys at a booth playing cooties. I was waiting for Ana who was in the bar covering for Mr. Wittson, who was discussing business with the manager of Falling Stars about playing at the pool hall in the end of June. Falling Stars was not my favorite band but the loud anger girl music excited a lot of teen girls.

"You're on" Adam took my order pad.

"Yeah" I roll my eyes.

"You don't like it?"

"I love playing, I don't like that" I pointed to a group of record producers. They were there every week and every week Uncle Marc told them no.

"Dad hates them too; he says they don't get it."

*　　　*　　　*

After the pool hall closed for the night, Uncle Donavan finally let Colt and Lorenzo stop cleaning with promises of more tomorrow. I couldn't sleep so I watched Ana sleep. Morning came fast; Paul came up around seven thirty "Morning monkey man."

"Uncle Danny says I don't sleep enough" Paul crawled in between Ana and I.

I laughed "Want breakfast?"

"No, Mommy" He curled into Ana's arms and went back to sleep.

At eight I couldn't take it any longer and just got up. After my shower I downed about three fourth jug of orange juice. The note said Mama had taken Christian to breakfast. Uncle Don already had Lorenzo and Colt cleaning. Anthony was watching cartoons with Nick.

"You look awful" Uncle Danny said.

"I didn't sleep" I yawned.

"Going to share?" He indicated the open jug of orange juice in my hand.

"Oh yeah um sure" I handed over the jug, grabbed four oranges an apple and a banana and plopped down in the recliner. Anthony crawled in my arms with a stack of picture books.

"Want me to read to you?" I shifted him.

"I want to read to you" He smiled snuggling closer.

"OK"

"Daddy are you sick? You don't look so good."

"I'm just tired."

I listened to Anthony read helping him where he had trouble. Paul woke around nine with a fever, crying hysterically and pulling his ears again. So Ana called her Uncle; Paul had another ear infection it was like they would go away with the medicine and come back the second it was gone.

"Paul always gets ear infections" Anthony told Dr. Wittson.

"Always?" Dr. Wittson smiled "Does he get sore throats too?"

"Yeah but I think that's from the screaming."

Paul was trying to pull his ears off so I picked him up, rocked him and put an ice pack to his ears "Amoxicillin right?" I asked.

"Yes," Dr. Wittson answered "But also this is a referral to a specialist. He might need tubes in his ears and or his tonsils out. It's nothing major I had it done when I was little so did Ana, Kenny and your mama."

"Is that why Mama is half deaf?"

"No that is why she is only half deaf and not completely, if your Eustachian tubes are blocked it causes pressure on your ear drum this can cause pain, hearing loss or in some case the ear drums to rupture. Sometimes it is just a block other time like in my ears your Eustachian tubes form too small most times it takes one set of tubes other times like with your mama it took more than one set in fact it took four sets and a fifty percent chance she wouldn't hear at all. Breathe I am sure Paul will be fine I am having trouble with the inflammation telling weather it is just a block due to infection and or sinuses or if it is truly too small tubes that's why the specialist because no one should have this many ear aches back to back.

"Oh" I nodded a little worried.

"It's a very common procedure nothing to panic over, I see that look. Just call and make an appointment and go from there."

I nodded.

Ana laughed "Don't worry Uncle Kyle we will."

"Uncle Kyle, can your baby come play?" Anthony asked.

"K.J. Is a sleep, he will play more as he gets older" Dr. Wittson smiled.

"Oh ok" Anthony went off to his room.

"He has adjusted well."

"Thank-you sir" I mumbled.

"Are you ok? Are you getting sick?" He started looking in my ears.

Ana laughed "Al forgot to sleep again."

"Try chamomile tea or warm milk or try clearing your mind right before bed." Dr. Wittson said on his way out.

*   *   *

Mama took Christopher to lunch, the twins looked so lost separated; it was hard not to laugh as I watched Christian wander around aimlessly. Paul napped and I let Christian take Anthony outside so he would stop looking lost. I for the first time in a long time I got to curl up on the couch and watch T.V. just Ana and I.

"Take a nap" Uncle Christian laughed from the kitchen, the fifth time I caught myself dozing off.

I woke around four; the notes on me said Ana had taken the boys to dinner with her father, Mama had taken Colt to a movie, and that dinner was cooking. I looked at dinner beef stew in the crock pot, it smelt incredible. I did laundry, cleaned up my room and the bath room in my room. Mostly the tooth paste mess Kenny was for ever leaving there. After that it was finally dinner, Lorenzo looked almost as tired as

I was. Colt was going on and on about the movie, Nick had his nose in a book, and my uncles were talking about soccer.

Mama smiled at me "How was your day?"

"Relaxing" I smiled.

"I hear Paul is sick again?"

"Another ear infection, he has a referral for some specialist."

"Dr. Campbell? He was great with Kenny's ears. Christian let go of his head, as I was saying he is a great doctor really good with kids."

I looked "Yep, Dr. Campbell."

"Good Christian won't cause a riot about proper child care."

I laughed; Uncle Christian was extremely picky about how he felt things should be.

After dinner I did school work, when Ana brought the boys back we played cooties and chutes and ladders with them then put them to bed. Anthony had only a fifteen minute tantrum instead of a full half hour one and I took it as a good sign.

Ana and I went to our room I was exhausted and she had homework. I read until I passed out and slept all the way through the night.

CHAPTER 14

Genevieve greeted me at the front desk Monday morning" Paula says you played with your mama's band!"

"Not now, Genevieve I will see you at breakfast" I was carrying a wild Anthony and Ana had a sleeping Paul.

"But I . . . Dog Breath, wait up" She ran after me.

I set Anthony in the time out room; he was still thrashing around yelling.

I took Paul from Ana so she could clock in, grabbed Genevieve's arm, and hauled tail down to the classroom hall. "After class I promise, at lunch" I ran to the cafeteria to grab Jupiter and Britney.

"Late much?" Brittany clucked her tongue.

"Yup, now move!" I wasn't in the mood.

"B . . ."

"Hush, get in class" I got them into class and ran to get a now claimer Anthony. "Class, love you, see you at lunch."

Paul and I collapsed in the hall between the classes. Paul was amazingly, despite the rushing back and forth still asleep.

Greg looked down at me "Give me the baby?"

"I got him" I rubbed Paul's back.

"Give him over," Dave's taking him to his office."

I sighed "Tell him thanks"

"Ooff what are you feeding him?"

I laughed "Grill cheese."

*   *   *

"You play at the pool hall!" Genevieve promptly accused.

"Yes, yes Genevieve, I do" I laughed.

"Paula saw you Saturday."

"I bet she did."

"I want to watch you."

"Friday and Saturdays."

"Andy won't let me yet; my consolers say I am not ready yet."

"When you hit transition you and Andy can have a private show. And when you leave here I will get you front seats for all the label bands."

"Not fair" Britney whined.

"He would do for you too if you ever let him" Tiffany snapped, playing with her gay pride necklace.

Jared looked nervously at the girls.

"Anyway" I said "If you get out before June thirtieth you can see Fallen Stars."

All five girls at our table blew my ear drums out.

"Thanks a lot Williams" Jared grumbled.

"Sorry" I rubbed my ears.

"What about me?" Amelia asked.

"Fall . . . that band is playing at the pool hall June thirtieth and July first."

There were more squeals.

"Daad!" Anthony objected covering his ears.

Really" Jared agreed.

I laughed.

"How do you work there?" Jupiter stared at his food.

"Headphones and years of practice" I laughed.

At two I took Paul to the ear, nose and throat doctor. Ana had fussed at me about making sure I got all the information. I filled out a stack of paperwork, they poked at Paul and set a date for the following Thursday to put tubes in. He was proud and told it to everyone several times.

"So what did the doctor say?" Ana asked me that night before bed.

"Um, he has surgery next Thursday" I smiled at her sheepishly.

"Al" She sighed.

Tuesday, Wednesday, and Thursday went fast. Up, work, home, time with Paul, bed; with few variations. Tuesday was the beasts' piano concert, Wednesday I broke up so many fights all four time out rooms were full and another was needed. It caused me to nearly forget counseling or well made it easier for me to try and skip.

"Let's go" Dave had me by my sleeve dragging me making the kids laugh.

"Dave I am busy trying to find a time out spot for Genevieve."

"It will wait . . . wait Genevieve what did she do?"

"Go look at Latrice."

"Genevieve my office now, Al consoling now."

I sulked down to the conference room where Charlie was waiting.

"Morning, let's talk about work" Charlie greeted me.

*   *   *

Thursday was awful Paul swore it was Friday and that I was hiding Anthony. I was never happier to see Friday morning. Once again Genevieve met me at security.

"Are we going to make this a daily routine?" I set Paul down.

"No, I am doing the mature thing."

"Um I will go with I appreciate the maturity after Wednesday, but I assume there is more."

"GET ME A NEW ROOMATE!" She began to cry.

"Yep thought so, same as last time?"

She nodded crying harder.

"No cry me Den O vieve" Paul hugged her leg

I had to look skyward not to laugh.

"Hey Casanova, I thought we had a deal" Greg laughed at Paul.

"Oh yeah, I be back me Den O vieve." Paul bolted toward the D-hall.

"Thanks a lot "Ana shoved Greg playful as I took off after Paul.

"Stupid medic" Genevieve muttered half smiling through the tears.

Half way through the C-hall I tripped and went sliding on the high wax floor landing sprawled against Bruno's office door.

"Giddy up daddy" Paul giggled crawling onto my back.

"Nnn" I managed as Paul's foot went into my face.

"I think you're backwards on your steed there cowboy" Bruno laughed picking Paul up.

"Ugh thanks Bruno" I pulled myself up.

"How did you hit my door?"

I pointed to the trip wire between C-4 andC-5.

"Sorry Trenton and Leshawn they aren't happy with me. That is three in a row, why does he keep taking off on you?"

"Greg, pays him to in tootsie pops" I scowled.

Bruno laughed "Have you even clocked in yet?"

"Are you kidding me, Genevieve has a new habit of cornering me at the gate."

"Here I will take him to Dave, you go clock in."

"Thanks" I got my balance stepped over the trip wire and jogged back down to clock in; grabbed Genevieve from Ana, I looked at the clock and took five minutes to comfort her. Her roommate had spent the week trying her best to make Genevieve attack her or herself. Wednesday Genevieve did attack; so badly that Latrice needed stitches. Latrice had started attacking Andy and Genevieve's sexual orientation.

Once I reported Latrice and got everyone in the family room, we were running fifteen minutes late. Bless Will; he and Cart were already there.

"In without killing one another go and sit down, I need to speak to Will."

Lynn rolled her eyes, Tiffany took Paul, and Genevieve dragged Britney by the back of her shirt.

"Rough morning?" Carter asked

"Better than Wednesday, today just started with a trip wire."

He raised an eyebrow "To each his own."

Will swatted him "So what's up?"

"Undercover cop?" I asked.

"Yup, yup, youngest on the force" Will smiled.

"Thanks again."

"Just doing my job."

"Eighteen and already a cop" I shook my head.

"I graduated at sixteen and went straight to the academy, my Dad was a cop. He died last year heart attack" He laughed.

I nodded

He laughed "You need a desk job, Al; those concussions are getting to you."

*   *   *

By noon Lynn and Brittany were back in there room, Jupiter was in his counselor's office, and Kyle and Kevin had left for the weekend. Tiffany was playing with Paul and Anthony and Genevieve was up on the bookcase.

"Come down please?" I asked her.

"Why?" Genevieve stuck her tongue out at me.

"Andy will be her soon."

"How do you know?"

"It's just about one."

She jumped down "There."

"Thank you."

She took her book to the couch.

I sighed

"Bad day?" Ms. Myers asked

"Nope, just thinking"

"When does Paul start preschool again?"

"February 26."

"Ok, how is Anthony doing with his weekend visits?"

"He loves it; I think he's getting frustrated with the Lego's right now though."

Anthony was growling at one of his Lego sets from his bin.

She laughed.

*   *   *

"NOOOO" Paul screamed from time out.

"Can you make him stop?" Lorenzo was doing homework.

"Hush" Uncle Christian growled at him.

Mama swatted Uncle Christian and placed sound blocking headphones minus music on Lorenzo's head. "There now do your homework."

"You're Beatrice" Anthony laughed.

We were playing guess who "Yep."

He giggled more "You can't be a girl."

"It's just the card I drew" I said. "Ok time to pack up."

"When will Grandma be back?"

"Um in eleven days."

"I miss her.'

"So do I; more than last time."

"Last time!" His eyes got huge "She leaves a lot?"

I laughed "At least once a year, book tours."

"She comes back right?"

"Of course" I laughed "In fact tomorrow after karate we have to go get her birthday present."

"Oh ok" He looked lost.

I smile "She will be back and I am sure she misses you too."

"Are we spending the night at Uncle Davie's again?"

"Nope sorry tonight Uncle David has to work with us. There is going to be a lot of people this weekend, don't forget your headphones and please help your brother pack, we don't need a repeat of the cooties and goldfish flying all over the kitchen because he forgot Teddy."

"OK"

*   *   *

It was like almost every teen on earth was in the pool hall or in the parking lot waiting to get in. Uncle Donavan was at the door carding and acting as a bouncer. The free standing tables had been moved out back under a tarp and the pool tables moved to the back half of the room near the bar. It was sixteen and over only tonight; so Colt and Lorenzo were working in the kitchen, Nick was at a friend's house, and Jr. and Jeremiah were outside helping Uncle Don. The Giant Ants were a death metal band. The twins were ecstatic, K-4 and Adam were practically drooling on themselves; they all got signatures, posters, and other stuff from the merchandise table. The merchandise table was outside and I bought two t-shirts; one for Kevin and one for Kyle, then got them signed. Kevin had, had a full month of good behavior without landing in the time out room and Kyle was looking at level 4 within the next week.

I know I told my son to grab his headphones, but I should have grabbed mine. I was bartending with Sam and Ana; they were why in needed my headphones. The twins were busing and Kenny and K-4 were waiting; despite the dancing screaming people and lack of round tables there were still ten booths and six pool tables to serve. The carding at the bar was ridiculous; I confiscated four fake I.D.'s. On top of that the confined space was starting to get to Sam and Ana.

After the band played, they went to the heavily guarded booth we had taped off for them. They signed things and when the crowd died down they wanted to talk to "M2CJ". I tried to stay working, but apparently Mama felt sitting with her was better for me; as Sam and Ana had started to "accidently" hit each other. I had checked on the boys, they were asleep and the other two were still cleaning. The guys in the band were around twenty-six or twenty-seven and asked Uncle Mark a lot of questions about when he toured.

*   *   *

The next morning I woke dazed after a really weird dream, I showered and called Mom before karate "Hey Mom, do I have a sister somewhere I should know about?"

"What? Alex, have you lost your mind?" She sounded like I had asked her to eat cow manure.

"I had a really weird, vivid dream that was almost a memory."

"Explain and tell your brother not to yell I can hear him."

"That's sad Mom, he's in the bathroom and I am in the boys' rooms trying to convince Paul that wearing clothes is the way to go; anyway it was me, you, Dad, Colt, and a girl we were at Grandma's and she told you we had gotten big."

"Are you sure it wasn't Ana or Jasmine and that's defiantly a dream all you're . . . ."

"I know but it was really weird."

"I bet and you don't have a sister I promise. What did we call the girl?"

"Laci, I was twelve, she was five and Colt was an infant. You and Dad were married and I spoke perfect English."

"Wow" She laughed, "That is a dream you speaking clear English at twelve. I believe twelve was the year you tried to make us move back to Italy by only speaking to us in Italian."

I laughed "That was ten actually, I think. But yeah it was creepy realistic."

"Well, realistic or not I did not marry your father and you have brothers so that's all dream."

"Did you ever consider dating . . ."

"Al, I love your Mama, I never considered any other person than her."

"But you're . . ."

"Fine go with I was never attracted that way to Colt or Christian." She laughed "I like blondes have you seen your mother lately. I love her, only her, now I have to shower and get to my signing and you have to get to karate."

"Ok Mom, love you, see you Wednesday" I hung up.

Colt stood in the door way "Ooo you bugged Mom at work, I'm telling."

I rolled my eyes watching him try to tattle, it obviously didn't occur to him that I had asked Mama for the hotel number myself after telling her about my dream.

"I has clothes, Daddy" Paul tugged my leg.

I sighed and laughed "Oh my silly boy, let's see if Nana can help."

He had put all four shirts on under his favorite overalls and on top of too. He also had unmercifully tangled himself in the shirts and buckles. Uncle Christian took a picture and sent it to Mom. I got three of the four shirts off and the buckles untangled, Anthony just sat laughing.

"Daddy, my oderalls has a boo-boo" Paul frowned.

I laughed "Don't worry they are fixable."

Mama fixed his overall buckle, then with the exception of Colt, Lorenzo, and Uncle Donavan we went to karate.

*   *   *

"Daddy what about this?" Anthony held up a dress.

I laughed "Grandma doesn't wear dresses, but that is pretty."

"What about jewelry? Great Grandma wears jewelry."

"But Grandma doesn't" Ana frowned "Your mom is hard to buy for."

"I still say we go to Michaels" I said "Watercolors."

"I was hoping for something different" Ana sighed.

I shrugged "It's what she likes."

Michaels was a bad idea with Paul, he had a melt down after trying to throw Styrofoam balls everywhere. Ana took him to the car while Anthony and I picked out paints and canvases. Anthony was looking at a craft kit of motorized cars.

"Would you like that?" I asked him.

"I have toys" He looked at his feet.

I the grabbed a car kit and a wooden fire truck with paint for Paul. Anthony looked at the fire truck confused.

"He will get it Monday when he remembers how to behave."

"Oh" Anthony scrunched his nose.

Anthony held the car kit all the way home; Paul was mad, jealous and still throwing a fit. He went straight for a nap. While Ana did our laundry Anthony and I built his cars. He took great care painting the frames and putting the decals on. The note on the table said Mama had taken Uncle Christian shopping, Nick was at Mag's, Kenny at work, the twins at work and since Uncle Don still wasn't home he still had Colt and Lorenzo at the barn.

No one had chores until Colt and Lorenzo were off punishment. Colt would probably be coming out of that faster, seeing as Lorenzo wouldn't stop talking back. So I left Anthony to paint and played a video game, and did some on line class work. Around four Uncle Danny came in, I thought he had left.

"When's dinner?" He asked.

I pointed at the calendar afraid to answer.

He swore "I will eat at Marc's."

I pointed at the calendar again.

"For crying out loud, just say it."

"Uncle Marc will be at Grandma's too."

"Right" He sighed.
I looked at him.
"Your mother scares me."
I laughed

*   *   *

Dinner at Grandma's nearly made us late to the pool hall and was massively explosive. Mama lost her temper several times; Uncle Marc and Uncle Mike didn't seem to notice or care until I tried to ask Mama why she and Grandma fought so much. At the pool hall it was blessedly less packed than the night before. The first two sets had gone well and with it not being overly packed I spent the down time reading to my boys. The third set was chaotic. Jr. got into a fight with some other kid and the "you don't hit my brother/cousin" mentality caused my brothers, cousins, K-4, and Jeremiah to join in.

The music and sound stopped; we jumped off the stage. I grabbed Lorenzo "Oh no you don't you are in enough trouble. Go back to work." Thankfully he listened and I was able to grab Colt whom chose not to listen. I had to drag him outside and toss him in a snow bank. Mama sat Christian right beside him and I heard several other thuds suggesting Christopher, Jeremiah, K-4, and Adam had been tossed in a snow bank also. Jr. was being pinned by Uncle Marc and Mr. Wittsom had the other boy by the ear. Jr. was screaming and trying to break free; the other boy was laughing.

Mama looked at my brothers "Back to work."

They obeyed, Adam, K-4, and Jeremiah went too.

"What happened?" Mr. Wittson growled at the kid he had by the ear.

"Stupid girly boy . . . ."

Jr. started to scream obscenities again; Uncle Marc shook him getting a better grip.

"Jr., care to share what happened?"

"I HAVE A GIRLFRIEND!" Jr. yelled.

The kid laughed again.

Mr. Wittson was losing patience "I can call my father-in-law or you can tell me what happened."

"Ooo I'm scared" The kid laughed.

"Officer Demin, stupid" Jr. tried to kick free.

The kid shut up.

"Now" Mr. Wittson growled "What happened?"

"HE KISSED ME!" Jr. yelled

"So you hit him?" Uncle Marc raised an eyebrow.

"No I told him I was with Sasha and he would have to wait his turn" Jr. blushed "He kisses good."

"Who hit first?" Uncle Marc sighed shaking his head.

Mama laughed.

"Him" Jr. screamed flailing his arms.

"Fine tonight you go home," Mr. Wittson shook his head "In the future don't hit what you want to kiss and don't kiss someone unless they want to be kissed. Jr., go finish your work."

My uncle shook his head.

Mr. Wittson laughed "That kid reminds me of Henry."

"My son's a moron."

"Just like you."

Uncle Marc laughed as well as Mr. Wittson.

*   *   *

We took the boys to the stables. Colt and Lorenzo were still cleaning horses and mucking stalls. So we just took the boys up with us on our horses. Anthony went with Ana and Paul with me.

"Not a me size horsy" Paul looked at caramel as I put the saddle and reigns on both horses.

I laughed "No, these are horses not ponies."

"It's looting at me."

I laughed "That's caramel" I handed Anthony the lead to caramel. "Walk her to Ana."

He looked at me.

"Don't worry, you can do it."

"Me do me do" Paul said.

"Here Paul, help me with Thunder bolt" I handed him the lead and grabbed thunderbolt's bridle.

Ana took pictures sending them to everyone she could think of. Ana took Anthony over the smooth trail; while baby Evil Kenevil and I went over my normal trail with the hurdles.

"Faster daddy, faster" Paul giggled holding tight to me.

When I was younger I used to randomly attack people taking pictures of me; now that I am older and there are less people trying to blind me with camera flashes I only attack one out of ten. The camera flashed and scared my horse as we went over a hurdle. I was about to start yelling when the stable hand grabbed Thunderbolt's bridle. "Sorry Al, are you and Paul ok?" He patted Thunderbolt's nose giving him an apple.

"What the hell where you think!"

"Sorry, Scot and I are taking photos for the horse show in July, I thought you were him he is riding Mystery."

Paul was clinging, I shook my head, "Here, hold Paul a second."

Hunter took Paul and I turned back.

"Paul stay with Hunter, daddy is going to give him a good photo."

Paul smiled, he liked helping Hunter. "Ok we takes your pit chur."

I road back and told Scot to grab Cookies 'n' Cream so that Hunter did not confuse anymore horses. If it had been Ana and Anthony something serious could have happened. Carmel was a rescue horse and neither Ana nor Anthony were as steady on a horse; let alone a spooked horse. At least if Scot had Cookies 'n' Cream I would worry less. I turned Thunderbolt around and we made a perfect run and jump, both him and I were expecting the camera flash this time and neither of us panicked.

Hunter thanked me and looked at Cookies 'n' Cream oddly.

Scot shrugged "It's a horse."

I rolled my eyes "Ana and Anthony are on Carmel."

"Ooh" Hunter nodded "Gotcha, no problem Al thanks again. Are you and Thunderbolt entering this year?"

"I don't know." We had entered all four years of high school but he was younger then.

Paul and I resumed our ride we met Ana back at the stables. After handing the horses back to Colt and Lorenzo we took the boys to the indoor pool and jungle gym. Paul napped on the way. Anthony wanted to swim first so I took him in the pool and Ana took Mr. Indecision to the playground after he stood there for fifteen minutes trying to decide what to do first.

Anthony swam well and liked the water. He said there babysitter had taught him, but not Paul because of Paul's constant ear infections, which made sense. At four we took the boys home in time for beef stew, bath and bed. I went over monthly bills with Ana. I paid my phone bill, rent for the week, cut a check for Paul's uniforms and balanced my checkbook. Once in bed with Ana asleep and Kenny not in the room yet I sent up a million silent prayers to be a good husband, a good father, for Mama to finally talk to me and most of all the bad withdrawals for no reason to stop.

CHAPTER 15

STATE WEEK

Monday I helped Dave, file and do paper work; it truly took from eight am to five thirty pm. My brain was numb and Paul was in bed when we got home, he had fallen asleep in his plate.

Tuesday I drew the short straw and had to show the state rep around. There were D.C.F. field agents in there every Friday, but for some reason once every three months they sent a rep for us to show around. I prayed that my group behaved, but even Dave wasn't sure they would.

"We have until noon then I have to take my group to lunch." I smiled at the guy.

"How many are in your group?" Mr. Polamnowski asked

"It depends on how they are doing, but never more than ten. Right now I have only eight. Today I have all eight at once tomorrow it will be broken down in smaller groups or one on one hours."

He nodded "Do all orderlies get about ten kids?"

I raised an eyebrow, Dave never called us orderlies. "Yeah, no more than ten; we normally work with the same set of kids every day, consistency."

He nodded.

I showed him each wing and specialized areas such as the time out rooms and the infirmary. At eleven forty five we went to Anthony's room, I explained that I had adopted him and I paid for private tutoring from Crimson Academy. Then we got Kevin and Kyle, they looked less pleased to see the state guy than Anthony. When we got to the tenth grade room Genevieve was waiting for us.

"Ancora (Again)!" I said; I refuse to ignore the kids for any state personnel.

Genevieve sighed "Latrice stabbed me" Genevieve was shaking "With her pencil. B-halls have pencils?"

"Um no one should in class. What did the nurse say?"

"I will live, just a small scratch."

"And Latrice?"

"She tried to say I stabbed my own back! All that lack of food has gone to her head!"

I held Genevieve well she cried.

Jupiter was first out the door "Uh-oh" He stood with the boys.

"Again" Lynn sighed "Can she at least walk and cry today I am hungry."

"Oh boy" Tiffany hugged on to Genevieve too.

"Really!" Brittany scowled "You need a new hobby, this one's annoying!"

"Brittany try some compassion, please" I sighed.

"Al, can I . . . who's the suit?" Tiny asked.

"No you may not just make Brittany disappear; and the gentleman accompanying us today is Mr. Polmanowski he is from . . . ."

"More state guys" Lynn groaned "Seriously Genevieve, I am ravenous today. Can you walk and hateraid melt?"

I sighed and lifted Genevieve "Walk, Lynn."

Tiffany didn't want to walk to far from Genevieve and Anthony didn't want to be too far from me. The state guy had a hundred and ten questions, bless the boys they answered everyone they could while I tried to keep Brittany and Amelia from fighting.

I flagged down Jared "How many you have?"

"Nine from A—hall" He sighed "Covering for Ryan. Quentin has Latrice."

Genevieve fell apart on me more.

I looked at him "Yeah, not a great idea."

"Um, she is level four."

"I carried her here; I need to file complaints too." I sighed and just held Genevieve through lunch. If I left my girls near Quentin and or Latrice I would have paper work on murder.

I returned everyone to class and carried Genevieve to her counselor. Then I went and filed a complaint and incident report. After that I went straight to Dave. I wasn't trying to ignore the state guy and was happy when Ana told me to do my paper work she had time to show Mr. Polmanowski around.

"Where's the suit" Dave asked.

I sighed "Dave you are as bad as the kids, Ana is showing him around. I want permission to take Genevieve with me tomorrow to Mama's pride rally.

"What happened?"

"It got moved so Mom moved her dates so we're al . . ."

"I mean Genevieve?"

"Latrice again, that kid's demoniaca (demonic)."

Dave laughed "Your Genevieve is no angle."

"I know she isn't, but she isn't stabbing people with pencils!"

"A pencil? How did Latrice get a pencil?"

"I have no clue, ask Quentin."

"Breathe, you can take Genevieve provided she is up to date on her school work, group, has no tests and does not have counseling tomorrow."

"Grazie (Thank-you)."

"You're welcome, and Alex, English!"

"Oops sorry."

"Uh huh, go back to work."

I found Mr. Polmanowski and Ana in the family room. She was explaining how this one was for the D and B-hall and the bins held personal items the kids could use under supervision.

"Everything well?" He smiled at me.

"Yes, sorry again, but to me the kids come first."

"I understand, you have a good day, Ms. Wittson here is going to show me to your boss's office.

I smiled hoping I didn't look too relieved and went to find Genevieve. I told her the good news.

"Will I . . ."

"You will be with me, call it a field trip or a vacation."

"I think I set my transition back" Genevieve frowned.

"Why, I'd melt a little too if Latrice was my roommate."

She laughed "Can you find out if I did?"

"I will do my best."

At five I spoke to Genevieve's counselor and then locked myself in the time out room. At five thirty Dave let Ana in.

Ana sat next to me "What's wrong?"

"I don't have a magic wand."

"For . . ."

I looked at her "I can't hurry a level change, control a person, or change the rules."

She stood up and offered me a hand up "Tell me about it on the way home."

"Um . . ."

"You'll be ok in the car too, I promise."

I looked at the mattresses.

"Trust me please."

I looked at her hand, for a second I thought of letting go then I stood up and we talked all the way home.

The next morning I had counseling so Ana went up with Paul and I would meet them later.

"How was your week?" Charlie asked.

"Good I guess, I did something weird." I played with my tie.

"Weird how?"

"Instead of staying in here and thinking the day out I talked to Ana about it on way home."

"How is that odd, she is your fiancée, couples share things all the time?"

"I never have."

"And she never asked you to?"

"She has, I just never did, or I told her I was just tired."

"Well, lying isn't good in a relationship. Communication is very important in relationships."

"I know. I'm just not good at it."

"Hmm, I have noticed. I see your mothers' stable is having a horse show and completion" He showed me the flyer with Thunderbolt and I as the main picture.

I smiled "That was Sunday; Hunter let Paul help with it."

"So you helped with this?"

"Yep, that shot was worth no panicked horses. That's my horse, his name is Thunderbolt."

"Are you entering?"

"I don't know, we ribboned all four years of high school but he is older now."

"Both you and him" Charlie said knowingly.

*   *   *

After counseling I signed Genevieve out; this time I remembered to let her get her street clothes and put on make-up.

"Did you find out if I set my transition back? Where is the rally? When are you returning me?" Genevieve said all at once.

"Wow, and I haven't even feed us yet." I laughed "You did not set your transition back, your moving back to your old room. There rally is in Mass. and I am returning you first thing tomorrow morning."

"Al, this is Andy's work."

"I know, Andy has your dress, it's my mom's birthday. Dinner is at a fancy high class restaurant."

"And they brought your brothers?"

I laughed "And my uncles."

Genevieve paced in the elevator like a caged animal; when we got to Andy's office Andy looked startled.

"Dress?" I asked.

She looked at Genevieve "Is she ok?"

"Perfectly fine, I'm proving a point to the management board."

"Ok" She hugged Genevieve.

I remembered Genevieve was a chocoholic-vegetarian and got her a salad and Hershey bar for lunch; I had a meatball sub. It was already overcrowded when we got to the rally. So I texted Ana, they were in the front row saving us seats. Genevieve was shaking, so I put my headphones on her and carried her to the front of the crowd. I sat her in between Uncle Don and I. Ana had Paul in a PFLAG shirt and handed me mine. His little cheeks said I love my grandmas' in rainbow face paint. I found the twins further back in the crowd for face paint and let Genevieve do her face, I was allergic to face paint. Ana had my banner it said: "Just because I am not doesn't mean I don't support." On one side and "I support gay rights" on the other. Mama got up and spoke about equality, unity, tolerance and diversity. She answered questions then finally cut the ribbon to the new LBGT center. There were some protesters but like most major annoyances less than when I was a kid. They were mostly extreme conservative churches that believed strongly in the old testament of the bible, and closed minded fools that were scared of their own skin. But the cops keep them back. I had read the parts of the bible that every one claimed homosexuality was a sin, not once did it clearly say homosexuality was a sin it said that people had created great sin and there were only seven deadly sins not one of them was homosexuality. I believed my Mama when she said God loves all his children. Genevieve had relaxed and was playing with Paul.

Ana gave me a disapproving look "How did you get her out?"

I grinned like a little boy up to no good "Dave."

"He spoils you" She shook her head. "She's not even on transition yet."

"She's fine, she will be transitioned on Monday her counselor is filing the paper work tomorrow if she is ok today."

"And if she's not you're setting her up to fail."

"No, I am not, she doesn't even know about this. I felt she needed a break before I fixed Latrice, Dave is moving her stuff back to Tiffany's room as we speak."

"I still don't agree with it."

*   *   *

At the restaurant Paul demanded he sit with *his* Genevieve. I hugged Mom, Uncle Chris looked exhausted. Thankfully my brothers and Lorenzo behaved. Genevieve was doing fine, she looked a little nervous, but ok. Paul tried to stick his tie in his apple juice; Ana took it away and told him if he couldn't behave there was no desert.

Back at the hotel we all talked and gave Mom her presents. I told her about work, counseling, Anthony and the horse show. She told me I should compete. Paul told her about his ears and his surgery tomorrow. Kenny told her about his computer science classes. The others shared school and friends. She told us about the tour I watched Mama and Uncle Chris play cards I was starting to think they never were away from each other very long. Mama told Mom about Colt and Lorenzo after we had all gone to our own rooms. The boys had two rooms and Genevieve had a room attached to Ana, Paul's and mine. It was connected by the bathroom. Paul thought the hotel room was great, he kept running back and forth between ours and Genevieve's until I settled him in the middle of our bed, Ana read to him.

I went to talk to Genevieve, "How are you doing?"

"Good now, your headphones they really help."

I smiled at her "I know."

"Thanks for bringing me."

"You needed the break."

"Why didn't you bring Anthony?"

"He had counseling and a spelling test."

"Oh, Al?

"Oh no you're calling me Al, what's wrong?"

"Why do I always want to cut?"

"It's an addiction; I have heard my mama say occasionally that she feels the pull. It's not that you have the desire to its how you handle it and the choices you make."

"And the Zen master returns" She laughed "I know, I know, you have told me this before a hundred times."

"Good night Genevieve."

"Night Dog Breath."

Seven feet doesn't fit well anywhere, but on a full size bed with two other people it just doesn't work. I tossed and turned and couldn't get comfortable so I made a pallet on the floor. Ana joined me trying not to laugh.

"Look Shorty just because you fit everywhere . . ."

She kissed me curling into my arms.

The next morning we had breakfast with Mom, she had to be in Springfield by noon.

"M-Mrs. Williams will you sign my copy please?" Genevieve yawned.

I tried to laugh but Mama and Ana swatted me.

"Not funny Dog Breath" Genevieve stuck her tongue out at me. "I love these books do you even read?"

Mama laughed "He reads when he's not passing out in the book."

It was only seven and Springfield wasn't that far from Boston but she wanted time with everyone and to make sure the boys didn't rack up a huge room service bill. Kenny had to be to work for nine and had rode up with Mama so Ana let him borrow her car. We took Genevieve back; I signed her in and stopped to hug Anthony I told him about Paul's ears. Then we took Paul for his tubes. They let us stay with Paul until he was out. I paced and panicked until they let us into the recovery room and he came to happy.

"Daddy that's not fair I only gots to tree" He looked around.

I looked at the recovery nurse, she shrugged.

"It's ok pumpkin" Ana laughed "We can count together on the way home."

The dr. gave us instructions on his ears and we went home. He counted to ten in English, Italian, and American Sign Language all the way home. Apparently he was offended he only got to count to three for the anesthesiologist.

"Feel better?" Ana laughed.

"I hungy"

"I am hungry, too" I agreed.

"How about some Friendly's, my treat?" Ana offered.

At home Uncle Danny had left a note saying he was at Grandma's for the night.

We tucked Paul in and went to our room.

*   *   *

Friday started with another bang this time it was the copier on fire, thankfully no one tried to escape during the fire drill. I got my group back inside before I realized Jupiter wasn't with us.

"Where's Jupiter?"

"Solar system has been in locked down since yesterday" Tiny yelled.

"Phew" I sighed, "Jupiter! Not solar system."

"Tired already Mr. Williams?" Ms. Meyers asked.

"No ma'am, head count after the fire drill" I gritted my teeth.

"Ah yes, fire drills are infuriating. Where's Paul today?"

"Ana and him are home today, he had tubes put in."

"I see; I will have to visit them at home" She went to speak to Anthony.

I nearly ground my tooth apart. "Genevieve come down" I sighed. "NO!"

"Please I need a new . . ."

"Battery, on it" She jumped down and took off.

"She seems happy today" Kevin's mom laughed.

"She starts transition on the nineteenth."

"That's great; oh and thanks again for Kyle's t-shirt he loves it."

"No problem, he earned it. I do for all of them they need to see we know they are trying and that we are proud of them."

*   *   *

Finally it was four thirty I signed Anthony and Genevieve out never wanting to see another D.C.F. worker lawyer case worker whatever again, even if *they were only doing their job* they were annoying and intrusive.

"Can I hear you play *now?*" Genevieve begged me.

"The paper said the nineteenth, so the nineteenth you can hear me play, the deal was once you were in transition. Right now I have to get you to Andy, Anthony and Paul to their uncle's and me to the Pool Hall to play."

"But I want to hear . . ."

"Night Genevieve" I laughed, Andy was waiting outside of the newspaper office for her.

"DOG BREATH"!

"Good night Genevieve."

"Not fair."

"The twenty third, Genevieve, I don't even have practice tonight." She pouted then hugged Anthony and I.

*   *   *

I couldn't focus, I kept calling David every chance I got to check on Paul and Anthony and I was running a fever.

"Al, go on break" Mr. Wittson took my order pad.

"Play darts with me Al?" Colt asked.

"Are you allowed?"

"I have an hour break. Are you still mad at me?"

"No, but I am disappointed in you."

"Play?" He changed the subject.

"I'll play but I'm truly no good at it.'

Mama liked darts and had taught us to play. I preferred pool and more importantly Ana, so I never practiced and then the cutting . . . well you know just certain people with sharp objects . . . Colt went first he was good, well better than me. His darts at least hit the dart board.

"Whoa there killer" Uncle Mike stopped my third throw.

Colt had picked up my first two darts laughing hysterically.

I blushed

"It's not a baseball" Uncle Mike laughed; he took the dart and showed me. "Now quit casting shadows and scaring customers we are on in thirty."

"Thanks Uncle Mike" I blushed.

Without even a glimpse of me having a chance at darts Colt beat me. He thought it was great, not even one of my darts hit the board. I was just happy that the stray darts didn't hit anyone. Colt went back to work and I went to the stage. Sadie was sitting with some guy at my drum set.

"To what do I owe this visit?" I shooed her off my drum set.

"Just a hug" she smiled "I'm here with friends"

"Okay" I laughed and hugged her.

Sadie looked like she was doing good; Tiffany had been sick and refused visitation on Friday.

"How's Tiff?" The boy asked.

"She's good."

"Al this is Wyatt my best friend." Sadie introduced the boy.

"Alex Williams, nice to meet you" I shook his hand. He had cancer awareness bands all up his wrist then I got a better look at him he had sunken in eyes and a ball cap on.

"Can I see her?" Wyatt asked.

"Yep Frida . . ."

"I'll bring you let's get back to Brandon, Jennifer and Ron. Bye Al" She pulled him off the stage.

I laughed "Sadie leave his arm on."

*　　　*　　　*

Saturday I woke up feeling mean and sat alone in the studio until it was time to grab the boys from David.

Ana came down first, "I thought so. Want to tell me what's wrong?"

I almost said nothing or I am just tired, but I stopped myself "I don't know, I woke up miserable and didn't wish to take it out on everyone else."

"Oh" she looked shocked that I didn't give her a one word answer. "Ok ready to go."

"Ye . . . no but I have to, we have karate, band, the boys wanted to go to Chuck E. Cheese."

"Al, are you regretting our sons?"

"NEVER!" I snapped

"Please don't snap at me, talk to me like a civilized human or not at all." She grabbed my hand leading me outside.

"Sorry, I don't regret nor do I wish to get rid of our sons, nor do I wish to cancel our plans. I truly don't know what's wrong."

"Ok" She frowned like she thought I was lying. "Are you tired?"

I looked at her.

"Yup, never mind."

"I . . ." This sharing my thoughts with Ana was harder than I thought it would be.

"Put your headphones on."

"I'm ok I just . . . do you think I'm a good father?"

"What of course you are. Al what's wrong? Did you have nightmares?" She stopped walking.

"You share a bed with me" I kept walking.

She sighed "Have you been digging again?"

I looked at her "Mom and Mama never left us with some . . ."

"We didn't just leave them with someone. We left a sick child with his uncle."

"We should have taken Anthony . . ."

"We gave him the choice."

"Morning" Ana's dad met us on their porch. "Am I interrupting?"

"Nope Daddy, captain paranoid just missed the boys."

"Daddy!" Anthony came out ready to go "Paul says if he has no fever we are going to Chuck E. Cheese."

I picked him up "You are going either way."

"Mommy" Paul yawned "Me too me too."

"You too, Pumpkin, let's get to karate first though."

*   *   *

Chuck E. Cheese was my least favorite place in the world. Even as a kid it was my least favorite place, but my boys seemed to love it. They had apparently made a plan; Paul grabbed Ana and dragged her to the playscape area, where the rat himself was talking to kids. Anthony dragged me to games.

"Ok, ok" I laughed as he pushed me to the water game.

"This is my favorite, I am great at it."

He wasn't kidding; he beat me forty out of forty times. It was the only game he played and every time he won the machine spit out ten tickets. I collected the 400 tickets and took him to Ana to play.

"Dad, Paul likes the sneaker basketball." Anthony said as he jumped into the ball pit.

"Um ok" I laughed and kissed Ana.

"They seem pre-coordinated." She laughed.

"Tell me about it."

Paul dragged me to the basketball shoe. "See Daddy this is *my* shoe." He crawled up on the step stool.

"Um ok" I put the token in.

"Backs up"

"Um . . . ?"

"*Dad,* in case I miss."

"Ok" I laughed.

Paul didn't miss and every time he got a basket the machine gave him four tickets. The machine gave him about a minute to shoot as much as he could. He averaged about ten baskets a minute. I looked at him.

He grinned at me.

"Ok smarty pants, what are you and Anthony after?" I asked after his third token.

He giggled "Choo-choo."

I looked at the display of prizes; on the top shelf was a glow in the dark electric train for 2,600 tickets. "Oooh" I nodded "Let's see what we can do."

We came up 300 short and brought ten dollars to Ana "Baby, ski ball?"

"I'm in the middle of tag" She frowned at me.

Anthony came to a halt when he saw us.

Paul looked at his feet "Sorry"

"You didn't win?" Anthony's eyes got wide.

"I Winned me shoe, it just stingy. Daddy bad at me shoe."

Ana laughed "Daddy is bad basketball, he likes soccer."

I blushed "Like or not I am bad at all sports. We are three hundred tickets short. Please Ana" I gave her puppy dog eyes.

"Please Mommy" Paul begged.

"Ok, ok" She laughed as the boys dragged her to the ski ball machine.

After we got the 300 tickets and the glow in the dark electric train I had the boys sit in the photo both while Ana used the rest room. We were starting a scrap book for Ana for her birthday.

*   *   *

We took the boys with us to the pool hall that night. It wasn't too busy but the boys still stayed on their cots. The first two sets went well the third set not so much, guitar strings keep snapping so Uncle Marc apologized and we called it a night. Clean up took forever my brothers and cousins fought and the main area was a large mess.

"What a pig sty" I shook my head as Kenny helped me clean up.

"Needs a leaf blower or maybe an atom bomb, then start from scratch" Kenny shook his head. Kenny was quiet and so well behaved that when he said things like that it scared me.

"Or at least less pigs on Saturday nights."

"How was Chuck E. Cheese?"

"Loud, fun I enjoyed playing with my boys, but it is loud."

He laughed "What are you up to tomorrow?"

"Stables, Anthony has been asking for Denim since Wednesday."

"How is he doing on the coming home?"

"Defiant" I laughed "He is arguing with everyone but his tutor, Dave and I threatening to hurt himself if they don't let him go home."

"Wow" Kenny looked stunned.

"I know, Ana and I have spoken to him about it with his counselor several times."

"Hey Al . . ."

"Yeah, Kenny."

"Thanks, I like being an uncle."

"Um you're welcome." I laughed.

*   *   *

Sunday Kenny and Juliette came to the stables with us; Colt and Lorenzo were still grounded; so Uncle Donavan still had them cleaning horses and stables. I checked with the stable hands to make sure there were no more random photos being taken. Then while Paul by his request stayed in the barn with Uncle Don, Kenny helped Juliette onto a guest horse and the two girls went riding. I started Anthony on the pony track with Hunter watching him. I decided that Thunderbolt and I would go out for the show and completion. Kenny rode with me making sure I didn't fall. I was rusty and fell several times causing my horse to come back and lick me; nothing said bad breath like a horses tongue.

"You need way more practice" Kenny laughed as we road into the barn.

"Unnn" I groaned "Don't remind me."

The girls weren't back yet, we dismounted the horses. I went to get Thunderbolt an apple.

"Loots daddy, me is king of me castle" Paul yelled "Just like *me* Den Ovieve is tween of her buot tase."

I laughed.

"I can jump like *me* Den Ovieve too." He leaped off the hay pile.

"PAUL!"

Uncle Don laughed at me as Paul landed a hay bale down and not on the barn floor. "Worry wart" He laughed at me more and went back to helping Lorenzo and Colt.

I stood breathing heavy holding my chest. As Paul hopped slowly down the hay bale pyramid one bale at a time and then back up. After I started breathing less abnormally, I checked to make sure Uncle Don didn't mind Paul longer and went to Anthony.

"Look Dad, I have the reins myself." Anthony smiled.

I took a picture "Awesome."

"That better be going to Ana's present" Kenny said watching Anthony with me.

"It is" I smiled "Like this, Bear" I straightened Anthony's arms and back.

"Oh" He focused on staying like I showed him.

"Oh Al" Ana laughed joining us.

"Yeah, I'm a bit more out of practice than I thought."

Kenny laughed "A bit?"

"I don't see you jumping hurdles."

"Nope I have a brain cell and a camera phone."

CHAPTER 16

"Sunday, Monday, Tuesday, Wednesday, Thursday, FRIIIIIIIIIIIIIDAY . . ." Paul sat the kitchen table singing Monday morning first in English and then in Italian, while Anthony had his Monday morning meltdown.

"Basta bambino (Enough, child)" Uncle Don sighed "That fit will not change anything you'll live and the weekend will come again."

Anthony just cried harder.

"Your Grandma will be home."

"Don, let him be" Mama frowned "See you Friday peanut."

"Paul we do not stick our nose in our breakfast; sit and eat appropriately" Ana sighed "Ready Al?"

"Yeah, love you Paul, be a good boy." I lifted Anthony remembering to watch arms and legs.

"See you tonight" Ana grabbed her lunch and the car keys.

It took me twenty minutes to buckle Anthony into the car. I hated being late to work but it took almost another twenty minutes to get Anthony in through the metal detector and to clock in; I forgot to grab his arms again and he tried to hold the metal detector bars.

"Rough morning?" Dave asked as I shut Anthony in the time out room.

"*You think*; he is why we are late. He refused to cooperate, he didn't want to come back and quite frankly I can't blame him . . ."

"Happy Monday Alex" Dave walked off letting me sputter.

*   *   *

"Better?" Dave handed me a stack of papers later.

"Yep" I looked at the papers.

"I figured you would be; they are counselor thought requests."

"I know that, this one is for Brittany . . ."

Dave laughed "You know you love them *all*"

"Riiiight, is it unintelligent to write she is a spoiled brat?"

Dave shook his head and pointed at the sheets "Two forty"

"Yes Dave "I sighed.

*   *   *

"Daddy . . . Daddy . . . Daddy"

"Paul . . . Paul . . . Paul . . ." I laughed picking him up. "What's up monkey?"

"I loves you" He giggled, he was in his PJ's fresh from bath.

"I love you too silly" I sat him down.

"Paul Robert" Uncle Christian growled.

Paul giggled and bolted into his room.

"Uh oh, sorry Uncle Christian" I said.

"He is three Al, early bed happens." Uncle Christian raised his voice loud enough for Paul to hear "And if he doesn't stop getting out of bed now he will have early bed tomorrow too."

I looked at his chart before I ate and groaned.

"I have seen worse" Mama laughed "Don't worry so much."

"He bit?"

"Yep, himself and Christian, it wasn't his brightest move. He bit Christian and your uncle put him in time out and told him he doesn't get to bite other people and in a moment of talking back and defiance he bit himself."

I laughed "Wow, my son's a genius."

"No he is three, and it was his way of telling your uncle off. They raged war all day. You have messages."

"Um . . ."

"That lady from the preschool would like you to call back and this" Mama handed me an envelope from the bank.

"Thank you Mama."

"You're welcome, also Andy called?"

"Um said she works at the newspaper . . ." Colt added.

"Oh that could be bad" I excused myself and made the call.

"Good evening?"

"My mom said you called" I choked.

"Who is this?"

"Alex Williams."

"Oh yes, sorry Alex, I had a question about this transition thing."

"Oh ok. She goes back to her old school Monday through Friday. You still have her on the weekends and she will be at the center when not at school or with you."

"She will still get her counseling yes?"

"Of course."

"Regular school . . . will she require money or supplies?"

"Nope she went to school today."

"Do you know how she did?"

"She did great, was excited about real homework and real books."

Andy laughed "Thank you Alex, have a good night."

"Night."

*   *   *

Tuesday was over before I was fully awake and Wednesday dragged after counseling as I filled in for someone in the A-hall. The A-hall work was mind numbing as only level three and up were aloud out of their rooms. Thursday was whine at Alex day and I nearly lost my mind. Finally it was Friday again.

Ana kissed me good morning.

"Did we remember to pick Paul's school uniforms?" I asked.

"Wow that's what my kiss did to you?"

"No sorry, I love you."

She laughed "Ok, dear, yes we did."

"Good, weird nightmares." I kissed her.

*　　*　　*

"Grandma!" Anthony flew into Mom's arms.

Mom had rode with Ana and I this morning, Paul had stayed home with a high fever and upset stomach. "How's my grandson?" She asked him.

"I'm good," He smiled "Come play Lego's with me."

"Of course" She accompanied him.

My head started to pound around noon; thankfully I only had Genevieve, Jupiter, Tiffany and Anthony. Brittany and Lynn were both in the infirmary with similar symptoms to Paul. And my other three terrors had already left for the weekend.

"I am taking him home" Mom declared.

"Ok" I laughed.

"Al?" Genevieve said from the top of the bookcase.

"Uh oh, what's wrong?"

"Homework, I have to write a paper on someone who has inspired me and what I consider good qualities in a person."

"Ok . . ."

"Can I use you?"

"If you feel the need."

"Thanks Dog Breath."

"Hey Alex," Tiffany mumbled.

"What's wrong?"

"My head" She cried "Everything . . ."

"Genevieve, please take Tiffany to the infirmary; I am calling a head."

"On it" Genevieve said.

"She didn't eat the same thing as Brittany . . ." Jupiter gave me a panicked look.

"You got it, go straight to your room or Genevieve's; I will be right there."

"But . . ."

"I promise between here and there no blades or going to jump on you."

"Um . . . I mean you look sick, too."

"Headache" My cell phone went off "Williams" I sighed "What? Sorry Mama, they . . . I will . . . ok, ginger ale . . . ok thanks Mama."

Jupiter looked at me "Al . . ."

I handed him my walkie-talkie "Take this, get to your room; tell Dave quarantine." I just made the men's room before lunch and breakfast made an unscheduled reoccurrence "Figlio di puttana" I cussed.

*   *   *

The weekend was awful; Paul, Anthony and I were all sick. Nothing was worse than a vomiting three year old. He cried and cried too sick to sleep, Ana and I took turns with Paul. Anthony slept, it was the only way he was comfortable between the killer migraine and the puking. I didn't blame him but when he did vomit he melted. Paul had trouble making it to the downstairs toilet in time in his panic, so we had him up in our room. Anthony was in Kenny's bed and Mom had Kenny sleep on Anthony's bed to keep him from getting sick, too.

Sunday Paul and Anthony were better I was not, and thankfully Ana didn't get sick. She spent Sunday bleaching our room and kept the boys on Kenny's side, once it was clean. Finally by Sunday night I was feeling better; not well enough for anything but crackers and ginger-ale but the headache was gone.

CHAPTER 17

MONDAY AGAIN

The weekend was so quick and hideous that it felt like I had two Mondays back to back. I had less of a fight with Anthony but I think that was because he was still not quite up to par, it was ok neither was I.

I put Genevieve on the bus and took the others to their classes. While they were in class I read the level upgrades. Kyle was level four, Tiffany level two, and Genevieve had moved to transition.

At noon I brought them to lunch and then back to class at one. Roger handed me a memo for an employee meeting on Thursday for all A-hall staff. At one thirty I got Genevieve off the bus.

"I have homework" She proudly announced.

"Ok" I laughed.

That was pretty much how my week went at work. At home Paul was seven steps passed excited. The preschool had called and changed the start date again for the third time, this time they had changed it to this Wednesday. Monday and Tuesday he was spastic putting on and taking off his uniform, packing and repacking his backpack and asking if it was time to go to school yet. Wednesday he came home with a pound of paperwork for Ana and I to sign and Thursday he came home with a painting for us.

Friday Genevieve's bus was late; she was very worried as she had an oral presentation in her English class first period. I assured her she would be fine, and that she wouldn't get in trouble for the bus being late. Dave had taken the wild ones to the family room for me.

"Dad where's Paul?" Anthony looked lost.

"School, they changed the start date again, he started Wednesday."

"Oh"

"Al my mom's here" Kevin said.

"Al . . ." Amelia called

"Alex . . ." Brittany yelled.

"Al . . ." Tiffany asked

Will laughed.

"Can I help?" Carter laughed "Al . . . Al . . . Al . . ."

I evil eyed him. "Now, Tiny they are here now, Brittany leave people alone and it is only 10:15 Sadie will be here around 2:30-3:00 o'clock."

"Skills come with the job?" Will laughed.

"Nope, you learn it or you lose your mind" I laughed.

"How's she been?"

"Her loving self" I smiled.

"Good, see you Monday morning."

"Ever feel like a child rental?" Kyle's stepdad asked, he came in as Will, Carter and Tiny left.

"More like a zoo" I laughed separating Lynn and Tiffany.

"Well so you know you are losing my animal; he and I are going to play hockey."

"Cool, have fun."

Brittany's dad visited her; I gave that man credit if I ever spoke to an adult like that I would have no teeth. Lynn's mother called and said she would visit her next week, she was sick. All the kids objected to another round of the flu. Jupiter's mother came with his stepfather and baby half-brother. It took all my energy not to say "I see why your dad got custody." At lunch I called home. No one had been up when I left for work and Ana had called in sick. She promised me it was just sinuses.

"Happy birthday to you, happy birthday to you Al is an ugly frog . . ." Greg sang loud and off key shoving a card in my face.

"Or you could just come to the pool hall tonight" I laughed.

"Oh I am; this is from Dave he's in meetings all day, so he had me give it to you."

I laughed Dave always gave me the best cards.

"How many times are you gonna call them before you get they aren't taking calls" Greg shook his head.

"It's not the same number. It's all numbers there's like forty of them."

"Way too many people" He laughed "Back to work I go."

At 2:15 Harry sent Genevieve down to me, complaining about the bus. Genevieve wasn't the only level four, just the newest and the bus driver almost forgot to let her off after letting the other six off.

"How was school?" I asked.

"I GOT PIZZA!"

I laughed "Glad you had a good day."

"Some guy hit on me and I was like um no, you're a guy and you're a freshman and I am already engaged and you're immature . . ." Genevieve kept going, I half listened watching Brittany try to pick a fight with Jupiter.

"SADIE!" Tiffany yelled in my ear and ran into Sadie's arms.

"Genevieve . . ." I asked.

"Tylenol right?" She beamed.

"Exactly" I sighed.

At four I brought them to group, grabbed all the birthday cards for Ana and I piled in my locker, signed out Anthony and Genevieve and took five minutes in the men's room to try and regain my hearing from Tiffany's squeal.

"Daddy where's Ana?" Anthony noticed we hadn't waited for her.

"Out with your grandparents, I think I can't reach anyone at home. I think it's my phone again."

"Oh . . ."

"Dog Breath where's Andy?" Genevieve looked confused.

"She is supposed to be meeting us at my house; I am keeping my promise you have a five thirty private show."

She squealed "No way!"

I accidentally swerved.

Anthony giggled.

"Oops, sorry Dog Breath."

"It's ok Genevieve" I said through my teeth; it was definitely 'squeal in Alex's ears day'.

"Oh and I almost forgot, HAPPY BIRTHDAY DOG BREATH!" She jumped on my back as we got out of the car at the base of the drive way. "Is that your house?"

"No" Anthony laughed "That's Uncle Kyle's; Daddy is he home? Can we visit the baby?"

"I think he is already out our house, we are pushing the clock." I put him and Genevieve on my sled and I got on Nick's and hit the buttons.

"Whoa" Genevieve clung to Anthony.

"Weeeeeeeee!" Anthony squealed.

"THAT'S *MY* DEN OVIEVE NOT YOURS!" I heard Paul yell as we got to the top of the drive way.

"Manners Paul" Ana corrected him. "Hey baby, how was your day?"

"Squeal-a-rific" I gritted my teeth.

Genevieve stood up and looked around "Wow that's a lot of sleds."

"Yep, can't use the driveway in the winter" I put the sleds away; Nick was always sliding down and walking up.

"Someone does" She pointed at the tire tracks.

"Uncle Marc's truck is a bit special." I hugged Ana and Paul.

"That good?" Ana laughed.

"We have cards" I handed her the stack addressed to her.

"How are you pumpkin?" She hugged Anthony.

"Hi Ana we brought Genevieve with us and its Daddy's birthday and all the girls squealed in Daddy's ears and why is Paul doing that?"

"Paul is trying to help, Grandma, make ice cream."

"Um . . ."

"I know" She laughed.

"Ok" I shook my head "I have to get in there I am going to be late, I still have to shower and change."

"Back door then" Ana laughed.

"Oh great" I rolled my eyes and ran around back, up the stairs, through the kitchen, living room, up the stairs and back down into the shower with lightening speed. Then I tried to slam through the front door but it was blocked from the other side.

"Front door, birthday boy" Uncle Danny laughed from the other side.

If this is what they did to Mama as a kid I know why she hates her birthday. "Arrrrg" I groaned running back out the back door, down the stairs and around to the front door.

"You look rattled dear" Ana teased.

"No one is letting me into the studio."

"Oh yeah that, we love you" She grinned and knocked on the door. "Ready in there?"

"Yup let him in" Kenny called out.

Ana opened the door.

"Happy birthday to you, happy birthday to you . . ." Everyone was in the studio and it was decorated; Mom and Mama were holding a chocolate cake.

I blushed.

"Blows them candleds out Daddy" Paul yelled blowing out half of them himself.

I let Anthony help me blow the rest out.

"What did you wish for Dog Breath?" Genevieve asked as I was helping Mom hand out cake.

"Wouldn't you like to know" I teased squirting whip cream in her face.

She licked it off giggling.

"Happy birthday" Andy laughed.

"Thank-you" I blushed.

After cake, presents, and dinner which was pizza, we had practice, We were playing "Rumor Mill" at the pool hall tonight so Uncle Marc felt we should practice it first as he felt Uncle Christian was probably rusty. Paul sat in Genevieve's arms refusing to give up *his* Genevieve and Anthony sat with his toys on the stairs.

"You whine and complain life's not fair, you say you can't seem to escape all the negative drama hanging in the air. You watch every one around you, jealous that they are happy.

Karma is an evil mistress, very hard to please, especially when you're spreading lies left and right all over town. You don't want the endless drama, stop your foolish ways. Spreading rumors left and right to make your day complete won't get you very far.

You whine and stomp your feet poor me poor me. Somebody help me yet when they need you your never around. I give and I give and you take and you take. Taking for granted my generosity

Karma is an evil mistress, very hard to please, especially when you're spreading lies left and right all over town. You don't want the endless drama, stop your foolish ways. Spreading rumors left and right to make your day complete won't get you very far.

You walk around as if you are perfect; with yourself imported air as if every ones beneath you prancing about on your negatively created personal gain sticking more swords in different peoples backs.

Karma is an evil mistress, very hard to please. Your throne of lies is getting hard to balance everyone is taking bets on the crash date. You have told so many lies that you can't remember what the truth is or where your loyalties should lie. All that energy spent on being fake no wonder you're so mean! Too tired to be anything but cruel!

Karma is an evil mistress, very hard to please, especially when you're spreading lies left and right all over town. You don't want the endless drama, stop your foolish ways. Spreading rumors left and right to make your day complete won't get you very far."

"YOU'RE AWESOME" Genevieve screamed jumping on me the second Mom and Uncle Chris stopped singing.

"Thanks" I laughed.

At the pool hall I didn't have to work just play when the band was on stage. Mr. Wittson had set aside two booths in the back for us. David had offered to watch the boys but I didn't want to be away from them; I didn't even have them in the back on their cots. There was never ending soda, shakes, chicken strips, and curly fries. It was nice to just hang out with Greg and Wilson; Ana had her friends too. Like when we were little the ice cream cake from Ana's dad said happy birthday Ana and Alex; Ana's birthday was two days after mine, the twenty fifth. Several older patrons gave us dirty looks for having the boys in their pajamas and with us at the table. I tried to ignore it and put it out of my mind; this was my birthday party and I wanted my son's with me.

Greg got me a new cribbage board, probably got tired of me complaining about my old one. Wilson handed me a huge pile of McDonalds' coupons laughed and then handed me new drum sticks and a gift card to the organic clothing store where Ana gets all my really comfortable t-shirts. I got new scrubs from the boys; Paul was highly offended that work dress code said they could only be navy blue. I got a lot of drumsticks and cash. My uncles gave me a see us tomorrow card. Ana got me a new pool cue it was sleek shiny black with pewter dragon inlays on it. Ana's friends got her girly stuff like lotions, jewelry, perfumes and gift cards.

"Hey, you never let me see the card Dave got you" Greg said.

"Oh, sorry the day got loud and busy and mostly loud. It had a wide eyed dog on the front it said 'He just saw the model I got you for your birthday'. On the inside it had a rather non anesthetically pleasing cartoon 'hag' and it said 'Did I mention she was half price? Happy birthday!'."

"Nice" Greg laughed. "Hey Paul I have three lolly pops that say you can go tell Mr. Wittson that I would like another milkshake."

"Ok, UNCLE KORK" Paul took off under the table before Ana or I could catch him.

I evil eyed Greg and took off after Paul.

"Wow, Paul's fast" Wilson marveled.

"That's nothing" Greg laughed. "You should see him move down and empty hallway."

Ana shook her head "You're going to give him a heart attack."

"Yeah," Wilson added "He is rather high strung, tonight, what gives?"

"*Tonight?*" Madeline rose her eyebrows "Every time I have seen him since we graduated he is wounded tighter than those drums he plays. Is he trying to quit smoking I know when my dad tried to quit . . ."

"Alex smoke? Are you on something, Alex would never smoke" Debbie cut her off.

"He's just worried about being a good parent" Ana sighed.

"Well that's stupid" Greg said.

"Uh-oh" Wilson pointed at me.

I had tripped and slid head first into the bar.

Paul giggled and climbed on my back "Giddy up Daddy."

"Whoa there monkey" Ana lifted him off of me "Not a horse right now."

Greg helped me up "Ok?"

"Ow, the bar is harder than Bruno's door" I laughed. "I'm going to kill you, if you keep doing that, at least give me the head start."

"Why so he has a running start at your back" Wilson laughed "Putting an empty fry basket on the counter."

"Mr. Wittson . . ." The room spun.

"Uncle Kork ice please, Al slammed his head" Ana said setting Paul on a stool.

"Anth . . ." I sputtered.

"Hush" Greg said looking in my eyes "How many fingers?"

"Where's . . ."

"In the booth asleep against my wife, I will file a sexual harassment suit later, but for now, your kid is right where you left him. Now answer, Greg" Wilson shook his head.

"Um . . ." I tried to focus on Greg's hand.

"Now is that um your I.Q. showing" Wilson laughed.

Some rather drunk lady at the bar gave Paul a dirty look "Children at the bar" She scoffed.

"Put a cork in it you old bat, dry out your liver would love it." Greg was not always polite.

"He's my son Ma'am, my family owns this place, he sits there spinning on that stool every time his father crashes head first to the ground" Ana rolled her eyes.

I tried to tell someone to get Paul back to the table and that Greg need to hold his hand still; but I just passed out.

"Happy birthday sweet heart" Ana laughed; Wilson and Greg caught me.

I came to in the booth with a flash light in my eyes and Greg and Dr. Wittson standing over me. "Where are Paul and Anthony?" I tried to sit up,

"They're fine" Madeline rolled her eyes.

The room spun and I grabbed the table "Where are the . . ." All the pizza, cakes, candy, chicken, and ice cream I had been wolfing down that evening came back up on Greg, Dr. Wittson and I.

When I came to again it was really quiet and I was yelling for my sons before my eyes were open.

"Whoa breathe" That was Mama but I thought it was Kenny.

"My kids?"

"Right next you, sleeping."

I rolled over I was at home in my bed "Where's Ana? What time is it?"

"Slow down, breathe, Ana is still at the pool hall it is only midnight."

"But we should be on stage."

"No you need to rest now; you hit your head really hard."

"No harder than normal, how did I get here?"

"You passed out twice; your uncles brought us home, and carried you up to your bed."

"Um . . . I don't remember anything past Greg asking me how many fingers."

"Yep, that's a concussion."

"Uhg." I groaned "I'm a bad parent I should give . . ."

"Do you really feel that way?"

"Like a bad parent, yeah I work all the time and I keep . . ."

"I meant that you should put them back up for adoption?"

"No, Kenny, I am selfish I love them too much. I . . ." The room spun.

"You rest for right now, you are a great parent, and we will talk about this in the morning when you remember I am not Kenny. And then again in several months when you have the hang of balancing them and the job as I told you before you are a good parent, Alex."

"No, Kenny I am a selfish parent and going to damage them."

"Ok, Al, Mama I am Mama, you need rest now night."

"Night Ken." I passed back out.

Mama sighed "Fool only thing he does badly is listen she tucked me back in went down stairs to Mom.

*   *   *

I woke the next morning with one hell of a headache; hand cuffed to Anthony. "Morning" I tried to say.

Anthony stared at me "Was that in Italian, Paul?"

Paul laughed "No."

"Morning" I said more clearly seeing that Paul was tied to my other arm, both dressed and ready for karate "Anthony?"

"You told Nana that you were going to give us back, last night" Anthony accused.

"Um . . ." I tried to remember "I can't remember last night."

"That's cause you go boom" Paul giggled.

I stood uneven trying to lift them.

"Oh no you don't" Ana came running out of our bathroom. "Boys what on earth . . ."

"Daddy is going to give us back" Paul stated.

"Over my dead body, that's just crazy talk." She untied me and handed me clean clothes.

"He told Nana, last night" Anthony objected.

"Daddy hit his head really hard last night; I bet he doesn't even remember saying that."

"Last thing I remember," I swayed coming out of the bathroom, "Is Greg yelling at that lady while sticking his hand in my face."

"See boys now go help your cousin load the van."

"Okays" Paul ran off.

Anthony looked at me "Do you want to get rid of us?"

"No of course not, I don't even remember that; are you sure it wasn't a dream?"

"Yes, Nana had just tucked us in."

"Well I am sorry, pumpkin, I don't want to and I don't remember saying it. Go help Lorenzo, your brother likes to tease him unmercifully."

"Ok" Anthony said.

The rest of the day I noticed him trying to be extra good; he scolded Paul for the smallest of things that Ana and I had never thought needed correcting. I thought maybe he just needed more one on one time with me. So I offered to play board games with him or taking him sledding but, he insisted he was bothering me and went to play in his room. Before dinner I saw him and Paul trying to pack and hid their toys.

"Boys what on earth?"

"We like our toys and Paul has . . ." Anthony started to say.

"Come to me" I lifted Anthony.

"Sorry Paul" He cried "I tried to be good."

Both Paul and I looked confused.

"You is good, Daddy said so" Paul unpacked his toys.

I took Anthony slowly trying not to fall down to the studio.

"Alex, Ana said you're not supposed to lift us anymore" Anthony said.

That stopped me mid step; I sat down with him on the steps. "Talk to me and she said not to lift you until I stopped getting dizzy. Now I may not be a therapist and my mandatory Psyche class is in teaching kids with special needs like Autism but I know when something isn't right."

"Autism, Hey, D-hall Dave Said that's what the really tall boy in the C-hall has and that he thinks his are parents are stupid."

"Dave can be opinionated, and I would prefer you would call him Mr. Ellsworth or at least Mr. Dave."

"D-hall Dave told me that if you said that we were to swat you but since I'm in enough trouble . . ."

"You're not in trouble, why do you think you're in trouble?"

"You separated Paul and I, and you're crunching me."

"Oops" I blushed "Sorry about your rib crunching, pumpkin, your great grandma use to hug me that tight when I took too long in between visits."

"I'm not in trouble? Then why would you want to give me back?"

"That's just it I don't want to give you back."

"But you told Nana you were a bad father and you want to give us back."

"Look, Pumpkin . . ." The room spun "Can you go get Nana or Grandma."

He ran up the stairs panicking "Nana, Uncle Chris, Daddy's green again like when he puked on Uncle Kyle."

"Shit!" I swore again, I had been doing that a lot lately. "I puked on Dr. Wittson, Mama?"

"Wouldn't be the first time," She laughed, "What's wrong?"

"My son insists that I told you I was putting them up for adoption."

"Well, you did, you also thought I was Kenny and you were in the bottom of the school swimming pool. Screaming hysterically for your sons every time I woke you; so I told you we would talk about it once you rested."

"Well, I don't remember it and I am NOT GIVING THEM BACK. THEY ARE MINE AND I WILL . . ." I had started to yell.

"Hush, let's put you back on the couch" She shook her head "And you go play, he loves you and no one's putting you or Paul back up for adoption."

"Promise?" Anthony squeaked.

"I promise, now go play."

I fell back asleep and when I woke again everything was silent and pitch back. My head was sore and tender but the headache was gone. The room only spun when I tried to think too hard so I got some food and went back to sleep.

Sunday I woke with Paul on my back "Giddy up Daddy."

"That sounds good, are you dressed?"

"Yeps"

"Is Anthony?"

"Mommy took him to Papa's."

"Ok" I stood "Let's leave a note for Mommy and Anthony."

I grabbed some food for lunch for the two of us and left the note. I didn't bother changing my clothes; I would shower and change afterwards. I didn't need someone telling Mama or Mom I was up and moving around. Paul and I made it to the bottom of the hill; Uncle Don's truck was gone as was Uncle Christian's motorcycle.

*   *   *

I thought they would be at the stables but they weren't. I took Paul on Thunderbolt with me we went really slowly.

"Daddy, Lizzy goes faster." He objected

"Daddy's head is still fuzzy."

"Oooh"

I took us five steps and my head spun. "Whoa, monkey lets um let's put you on Lizzy." I jumped down and carefully lead Paul into the barn. For the first time in my life I called for a stable hand.

"Mr. Williams, are you well?" Shaun asked

"Shaun, just call me Alex, can you please take Paul off Thunderbolt and get him and Lizzy set up for the pony circle. I need to make a call."

"Right away Mr. Williams."

"I'm just Alex" I called after him.

"Alex where are you!" Ana yelled into the phone.

"Don't yell baby, Paul and I are at the stables. It's where we hid your present."

"Ooh and I looked everywhere . . . stables! You better not be on a horse."

"I'm not Paul is . . ."

"Alexander Joseph so help me . . ."

"I am not Shaun has Paul on the pony circle I'm in the barn."

"Are you lying to me?"

"No, I'm in the barn I tried to ride but I got dizzy."

"ALEXANDER JOSEPH!"

"What, I got off immediately."

"WHAT?!? What? I will tell you what, you have a concussion you could have killed yourself. I overlooked you driving because you sound better but riding a hor . . ."

"Honey I am not riding I decided against it. Paul is on Lizzy in the pony circle."

"I don't care you tried to you stay right there I am having Daddy drop us off and we will drive you and Paul home."

"I just wanted to know if you had picked a restaurant."

"Yes, the ballroom café."

"Nice choice, see you when we get home."

"Alexander! You stay right there, Daddy and I are on our way. I get there and you're not I will concuss the other side of your head."

I laughed "Ok, ok, I am fine."

"Don't lie to me."

"I'm not; I'm trying to remember which cabinet I hid your present in."

"Ooo" She bristled "And that, that was so unfair at least last year you hid it where I could find it."

"I laughed harder "Baby you're not supposed to find it. It's not even fully ready yet."

Mom promised she would get me one last picture and that would be right before dinner tonight. I dug through all cabinets and hay bales, after hanging up the phone.

"Alex" Scott laughed "What are you doing?"

"Ana's scrapbook . . ."

"Under the sink behind, the Lysol in the plastic bag." Scott shook his head.

"Thanks" I pulled it out.

"Sir," Shaun led Paul and Lizzy in "Your fiancé has arrived with your older son."

"Thank you, Shaun, but again just call me Alex." I shook my head, Shaun was the newest hire.

"Alexander!" Ana stood in the doorway with Anthony

"Happy birthday, Honey."

"Is Paul done?"

"NOOOOOOOOOO!" Paul objected.

"Ready when you are" I smiled.

"Nooooooo!" Paul whined.

184

"That's nice Paul its nap time" Ana pulled him off Lizzy.

"Daddy, can I help put Lizzy away?" Anthony beamed.

"Let's let Shaun put Lizzy away today, I think we have to get home."

"Actually we have to stop by Aunt Kate's office and put this in the mail slot first."

"Nooooooo" Paul through himself on the ground.

"That's nice you're tired" I lifted Paul.

"You dizzy?" Ana asked me.

"Nope" I lied.

*　　　*　　　*

At dinner the boys were very well behaved. Ana liked the presents from my family and hers, they mostly lead up to the present from the boys and I. she squealed loudly disturbing other tables which got over it when they saw the baby blue and silver birthday balloons. I got a kiss that earned looks from her father and catcalls from my brothers.

I blushed "Um dance."

"I will dance with our sons; I love you but fast paced circles with a concussion . . ."

"Not funny" I swatted Kenny who was laughing like a hyena.

I sat with my uncles; watching my mothers dance and Ana try to teach Paul to waltz while Anthony watched laughing.

"You know, you screwed up your own birthday "Uncle Don accused "C.J., Christian and I have to wait to give you your present now."

"It's ok" I smiled "Watching her is the best gift in the world."

*　　　*　　　*

After we got home and put the boys to bed Ana excused herself to our room she had a report to do. I went to the roof.

"Coat" Uncle Christian said.

My coat landed on my head. "Hey" I sighed

Uncle Christian sat down near me "Want to talk about it?"

"I'm a bad parent."

"Why do you think that?"

"I nearly killed myself and Paul today."

"The horse?"

"Yeah, I think I over compensated."

"Explain."

"I was so worried about showing the boys I do want them that I put Paul on Thunderbolt with me and that was so dumb. I got really dizzy. I mean I got off immediately and had Shaun get Paul on Lizzy in the pony circle . . ."

"No one is perfect" Uncle Christian smiled "You know I was still putting diapers on backwards with Colt."

"Diapers aren't deadly or immoral" I sighed.

"Aahh" He nodded "No, no its not but your first motorcycle ride was at two weeks old with no helmet. My mother nearly killed me and so did your mother."

I laughed "You would never hurt me."

"Never intentionally, just like you would never hurt your sons."

"Well I seem to be screwing up left and right. The horses, letting Anthony hear something I don't even remember saying, and that lady was right I let them run loose in the pool hall . . ."

"So that's what this is about, that old bat at the bar; she has been sitting at that bar knocking back shots from 4:30 p.m. to close every day since I was a kid."

"The pool . . ."

"Small town Alex, the pool hall is open six days a week your parents used to work all six, that women had a son."

"So she doesn't have him in . . ."

"A safe place, you grew up in that pool hall your fine. Now hush I said had; *she era (had)* a son."

"Um . . ."

"Had as in no longer has."

"I'm sorry for her loss, but she's . . ."

"He didn't die Al, hush and listen. Ana's granddad got tired of finding the infant locked in her car on nights she couldn't find a sitter."

"He call the state?"

"No he called the child's grandmother and she took legal action."

"So you're telling me she's wrong to judge me?"

"Yep, and as for them running loose, they are not the first won't be the last. It is not a bar or a brothel it is a restaurant with a liquor permit, your sons are fine in there."

"Look how late I keep . . ."

"Are you still alive?"

"Yes."

"Do you think your mother is a bad parent, or your Uncle Mark?"

"Um . . . no."

"Then neither are you; don't take that women's words to heart. I think she was at least eight shots passed drunk when you hit your head."

"But . . ."

"But nothing, do you really think they are better off in the system?"

"No"

"Then what's there to debate, if the state felt you couldn't have provided a safe loving home for them you wouldn't have them connections or not. Don't worry so much."

"Did Uncle Mark make mistakes with Mama?"

"Letto (bed)!" He shook his head hiding a laugh.

CHAPTER 18

TIME FLIES

Monday I brought Anthony back but Greg had told Dave about my concussion so Dave said no work until Wednesday. Ana had a gynecologist appointment and Paul was at school so I went to the stables.

"Sorry Mr. Williams, Ms. Wittson requests I not let ride" Shaun said.

"Not riding, and Shaun just call me Alex."

"Um . . ."

"Is Hunter here?"

"Not yet sir, he is do in around four, sir."

"Thanks, Shaun, but please just call me Alex." I went home and paced around waiting for Paul.

Everyone was working, sleeping, at school or just plain not home nothing good was on TV, I had done all my homework, and there were still no chores as Lorenzo and Colt weren't off grounding until Thursday. I was restless; finally at 11:30 uncle Christian and Paul came in.

"And she said I was cooler than Thomas cause I has golded fish and . . . DADDY!" Paul jumped into my arms.

"Hi monkey, how was school?"

"Good, I has homework now bye-bye."

188

"Wait" I laughed "Let me see your stuff."

"Nots time yet, seeee" He pointed at his calendar "See sool, homework, lunch, nap, free time, dinner, bath, Mommy and Daddy, bed."

Uncle Christian laughed.

"I'm home early today."

"Ohtay, sorry Daddy I will talk to you at lunch I has to color my 'A'."

"Um okay" I laughed.

I sat the table and watched Paul color his 'A'. Then while Paul ate lunch he told me all about school and Hannah the little girl who liked his friend Thomas; and the little girl Cynthia who told him he was cooler than Thomas because he had gold fish for snack and Thomas only had apple slices. After he ate I put him down for a nap and napped myself.

Tuesday and Wednesday went the same. I'd put Paul on the bus and then get him off, watch him color or trace a letter, eat lunch and then put him for nap going half stir crazy. Tuesday morning Uncle Chris took me to get my motorcycle license then Uncle Christian brought me home four new helmets two child sized. After Paul's nap Uncle Donavan took me to a shed about forty minutes north of Hartford. Inside were two Harleys. He told me to pick one; he said they were my Dad's and it was about time that I owned one. Tuesday evening Dr. Wittson cleared me to work again. And Wednesday, morning, Dave had Greg double check me.

March went fast; I fell into a solid content routine. Around the first week of April I found myself waiting for Fridays and hating Mondays. Anthony stopped melting every Sunday night and Monday morning. Easter was a blast; the boys made it extra fun dying Easter eggs. Just there excitement over every little thing that was new to them or that they had never been allowed to do before. Around the end of April Anthony earned his yellow belt. The drive-way became full of bubble spills and chalk drawings. I spent Saturday mornings at karate and the stables in the afternoon before work. Sundays I spent outside teaching Anthony how to ride a two-wheeler and Paul how to ride a two-wheeler with training wheels; Ana took stock in band-aids.

May brought level changes at work for those who hadn't gone up in February and a new pile of surly level ones. It also brought the end of Ms. Meyers needing to visit us once a week. The closer to July it got more people confirmed that they would or wouldn't be able to attend Ana and I's wedding. Mom had to ban Colt and Lorenzo from answering the phones as they just seemed to get mouthier with each passing day. I found counseling actually was nice, it felt good to have a non objective person to talk to. I found myself spending less and less time in the time out room and more time talking about my day with Ana. Lorenzo realized he wasn't going anywhere and started to settle down, at least at school. I was getting more and more frustrated with Mama; she still wouldn't tell me about her past.

I blinked somewhere and it was June. The twins graduated both accepted into college Nick, Colt, Anthony, and even Lorenzo all moved up a grade. Paul was set to resume preschool in the fall. Ana and I both received our bachelors' degrees. The twins had a grad party and then Mom and Ana's dad against our protests had one for us. Ana had started to count down to our wedding and Anthony to the start of school again because he said he loved *real* school.

CHAPTER 19

EPIPHANY

Without me evening noticing it was one day and one week to my wedding. Everyone but Brittany and the two new girls, Carly and May, could go outside.

"It's not fair" Brittany stomped her feet.

"You're gonna graduate a level one, hell even Buddy and Curtis are level two now." Tiny clucked her tongue.

"Amelia mouth," I sighed trying not to laugh as Buddy had actually been level three for three years, "In your room now, Brittany."

"I can push her in" Tiffany offered.

"No thank you" I shook my head "Brittany, your room or the time out room."

"FINE!" She went in her room and slammed the door in my face.

I sighed and locked the door.

Anthony was holding a bucket of chalk, as always Genevieve had a book. Lynn, Tiny and Tiffany all had beach towels; they wanted to work on their tans. Kevin and Kyle had a basketball, and Jupiter had a sketch pad. I let them out into the enclosed play area. Genevieve plopped in the shade on a swing and was content.

"Alex" Tiny said "Tell us to roll in ten minutes."

"Um ok."

"So we tan even" Lynn laughed.

"Right" I nodded, watching Anthony draw, spaceships and rockets on the sidewalk.

"I am sorry to interrupt your thought process Alex, but you seem extremely distracted today. Are you feeling well?" Jupiter asked.

"It's his wedding" Tiffany yelled from her towel "He always looks like that when he thinks about Ana."

I blushed, "Yes wedding stuff, tonight floral approval, tomorrow gifts for ushers, bridesmaids, maid of honor, best man, Wednesday is paper work. Did you know there is blood work and paperwork with a wedding?"

"Well duh Dog Breath, it's a legal binding contract." Genevieve rolled her eyes "Just take it one day at a time like you tell us. Do you know if Dave mailed my college application yet?"

"I thought he did that back in May" I looked at my watch.

"It's 3:10, and yeah the initial one. You just got a degree, you should know there's not . . ."

"I did mine online; Ana went to a regular college."

"Well did he?"

"I honestly don't know. Kevin, watch the ball it goes outside the fence it's gone."

"Ok, Al" He called back.

I went back out into space and thankfully they behaved. At 4:30 I brought them in to clean up for dinner. I got Carly and May before Brittany as I was still in space. May did nothing but cry how unfair it was that she had to be here and Carly just gave everyone the silent treatment. Brittany on the other hand took my full focus on a good day and more on a bad day. Thankfully today was a good day. I opened the door to her room and almost regretted it.

"Its about time, I was ready to hit the emergency button and tell Dave you were not taking me to . . ."

"Shut up" Tiny groaned.

I rolled my eyes "Move or I will leave you here through dinner."

"Al, would you quit looking at your watch. It hasn't changed in the last thirty seconds." Jupiter held Tiny back.

"Sorry Jupiter, nerves, the girls haven't fought yet today. I fear it will bring on the end of the world."

"It might" He nodded "I asked what Thursday's field trip was; my counselor approved me to go."

"Oh um library, I think."

"Daddy" Anthony interrupted "Did Nana get my responses to my birthday party?"

"Yes Tristan, Joshua, Gavin, Jack, and Damien" I answered.

"Perfect! This is going to be so cool."

His birthday was on Friday, but we having his party Saturday at the planetarium. He had not made many friends in the two weeks before school let out but the ones he did make excited him. Finally it was 5:30 and I brought my level ones to group, my level two's to their room, Kevin and Kyle to the family room and Anthony and Genevieve to Dave.

"Five thirty already?" Dave smiled.

"Don't jinx it Dave, there were no fights."

"It's the fresh air" Dave laughed "How are they?"

"These two, fine?"

"Saturday we go to the planetarium for my birthday" Anthony beamed.

"Cool, Friday you and Genevieve leave here for the last time. So let's get you two to your group.

"Ok later dog-breath." Genevieve put Anthony on her shoulders and ran toward the group room.

"Bye Daddy, see you tomorrow" Anthony called back to me.

"I love you pumpkin, see you tomorrow" I called to him. I met Ana at the car. "Ready, let's get this done with."

"Wow, cranky much?" She frowned.

"Just tir . . . no I just want to get home to Paul. I am sure whatever flowers they have to arrange against the chairs are perfectly fine."

She laughed "I'm driving."

"Ok"

"Are you sick?"

"Nope"

The florist showed us five different things and Ana picked her favorite; then we left. At home I walked into the smell of chicken parmesan and fighting boys.

"I told Jupiter the apocalypse was coming" I laughed grabbing Lorenzo "You ok Kenny?"

Kenny was in the living trying to pin Nick "Do you know how this started?"

"Nope just walked in the front door, you?"

"No I came in the back, was out with Mom and Paul in the garden."

Ana came in after me sorting mail from her father's "Uh oh."

"Just get Mom they are in the garden" Kenny sighed.

Lorenzo tried to break free, "You're not escaping."

Nick's nose was pouring blood and Lorenzo's eye was swollen shut. The food I smelt, was mine and dishes were half done with several broken on the floor.

"Uh huh" Miss Gabby said.

"Hi Miss Gabby, thanks for dinner. Hi Mama, I'd hug you, but . . ."

"Your perky are you sick" Mama asked taking Lorenzo.

"I am not sick, I have good news. Anthony comes home permanently Friday."

"Awesome" Nick said from under Kenny; who felt sitting on him was the best way to pin.

"How did this start!" Mom asked removing Kenny from Nick's back.

Nick pointed at his nose "That . . ."

"Swear free!"

"He threw those plates at my face."

"Clean it up, finish your chores and straight to your rooms" Mom sighed.

Ana and I ate dinner Paul came in covered in dirt. I bathed him, went over his summer library program papers with him and put him to bed.

Tuesday we took Paul to work with us, and took off the afternoon, to get the last few store bought things. Then we went to sign Anthony and Paul up for the summer programs, at the library and community center for their age groups. After that we went to the stables; the competition was Saturday and I had just about perfected the run.

"Alex" Hunter picked me up off the ground again "You have to hold his neck on the last hurdle."

"I'm afraid of hurting him." I sighed, feeding Thunderbolt an apple.

"You won't hurt him; you have formed a bond with your horse. I just watched that, you doubted him and he tossed you."

By time to leave, I was holding his neck just like Mama held her horse's.

*   *   *

Dinner was fedaccini alfredo, Paul refused to eat, he sat at the table refusing to even try one bite until bath time.

"He wouldn't try it?" Ana frowned.

"Nope" I sighed.

Wednesday was paperwork everywhere and Thursday was awful; the girls picked the library visit to fight. Amelia told me it was worth missing next week's field trip to the history museum.

By Friday Ana was ecstatic and I was nervous. At noon only Tiffany, Genevieve and Anthony were left with me. The others were either in their room or home. The strict: room or time out room rule was Dave's way of stopping the fighting.

"Al can we go outside, we know Sadie won't be here until . . ."

"Give me a little more credit than that, it's a little hard to sleep until noon when you have counseling at eleven." Sadie came in cutting Tiffany off and acting all offended.

Tiffany squealed deafening my ear drums.

"Has she been good Al?" Sadie asked.

"I suppose she has, Genevieve please take you and Anthony to your last group session then to pack all your things. Tiffany ten minutes that's it I have to go get release forms for those two."

"Say hi to Ana for me" Tiffany wagged her eyebrows at me.

I shook my head "Don't make me reconsider."

I got two sets of release forms, counseling time and date request, and staff sign off forms. Ana wasn't at her desk when I came out of Rodgers office so I just went back to the girls.

"Do you mind?" Tiffany scoffed from the couch where her and Sadie watching TV.

Sadie turned a very lovely shade of fire engine red.

"Kiss that good huh?" I teased "To bad I am back."

"Not fair" Tiffany grumbled.

"Don't you start, a deal is a deal. I will only be in Rome for two weeks; honey moons aren't permanent and I want a good report when I get back. Jupiter can't do it alone Brittany and Tiny would eat him for breakfast Monday morning and not spit his bones back out till I returned."

"Yeah, yeah" They laughed.

At four I had Genevieve walk Tiffany to her room, and then take Anthony to get their release signatures. I showed Andy to Dave's office, after changing into street clothes, as that is where I told them to meet us to get the last two signatures, Dave and I.

"So, Tuesday, you actually have me taking a day off work" Dave teased. "Last time I took a day off work you were so little you called me the same thing your sons do without questioning it and your mother told me I better show up or she would break every one of my kids out."

I laughed blushing "Yeah, Ana's excited."

"And what about you?"

"Nervous" I laughed.

"Where is Ana?" Andy asked.

"She had a Gyno. appointment."

"Again?" Dave asked me curiously.

"Yeah why?"

Andy laughed "Girls normally have those once a year unless something is wrong or they are pregnant."

"Oh" I shrugged "Ana is paranoid of cancer."

"Understood" Dave nodded.

"Daddy, Daddy, Daddy" Anthony came running down the hall "Look what Greg gave me and these are for Paul."

I smiled he had on the Burger King crown from Kevin, the happy birthday sticker from Kyle and tied to his wrist there was a big shiny singing balloon that matched the one Greg had got Buddy for his birthday three weeks ago. "Did you say thank you?"

"Si, where's Mommy."

"She had a doctor's appointment; she is meeting us at home." I took Paul's lolly pops.

"Ok" He smiled "Ms. Andy, Ms. Andy are you and Genevieve coming to Daddy's practice today?"

"Yes we are" She smiled.

"I have it on the down low that Bruno and Greg, have been slipping him candy all afternoon" Dave laughed. "Genevieve, are you ok" Dave asked her signing her staff sign off sheet.

"It feels like graduation, surreal" Genevieve smiled.

"Ok, If you need your consoler is here and so am I and so is Al, Al what are you doing?"

"Sorry" I had been standing behind Dave making faces at Genevieve to make her laugh.

"Ok well, three of you are now civilians, let's walk you to security" Dave smiled.

"Daddy, do you have the motorcycle" Anthony asked.

"No I have the car."

"Aw man."

I laughed "Nice try, not until your ten, we are not budging on that."

"No, Mom isn't" He pouted.

"Actually, that is me not budging; your mother wanted to put Paul on when I first got the bike."

At home I texted to make sure everyone was ready. When the text came back I told him; yes, Ana was home already. I opened the door and let him go in ahead of me. Christopher had a sign that read "Welcome home Anthony" and Christian had one that said "Happy seventh birthday Anthony". Ana and Paul stood in the middle holding a U.F.O cake as we sang happy birthday to him.

After cake, pizza, ice cream, and presents we had practice. Genevieve and Paul sat in there usually spot on the dryer with Andy on the washer. Anthony was outside in his new leather jacket riding his bike.

"Eighteenth birthday came and went but I was still a kid. Picking fights left and right, getting picked up by the cops every other night. I was headed fast down a dark and lonely path of no return.

I was a blessed mess, running loose with no control; I didn't care right from wrong. Had no goals other to than to live and die, no dreams for a better me. Then they placed you in my arms and right then and there I knew there was no turning back I had an epiphany. You were every bit me DNA aside. I changed my mind; I needed a plan a focused goal. I had to put the past in the past and be the best me I could ever be so you would know to be the best you.

Twenty one came and I hadn't changed a bit. Like an ostrich with my head in the sand. I was running blind. I knew it all and everyone else was wrong.

I was a blessed mess, running loose with no control; I didn't care right from wrong. Had no goals other to than to live and die, no dreams for a better me. Then they placed you in my arms and right then and there I knew there was no turning back I had an epiphany. You were every bit me DNA aside. I changed my mind; I needed a plan a focused goal. I had to put the past in the past and be the best me I could ever be so you would know to be the best you.

And then they placed you in my arms and right then and there I knew there was no turning back I had an epiphany. You were every bit me DNA aside. I changed my mind; I needed a plan a focused goal. I had to put the past in the past and be the best me I could ever be so you would know to be the best you.

I was a blessed mess, running loose with no control; I didn't care right from wrong. Had no goals other to than to live and die, no dreams for a better me. Then they placed you in my arms and right then and there I knew there was no turning back I had an epiphany. You were every bit me DNA aside. I changed my mind; I needed a plan a focused goal. I had to put the past in the past and be the best me I could ever be so you would know to be the best you." Mom sang.

I had never heard this song the sheet said it was called Epiphany "Mama did you write this?"

Uncle Marc shot me a look I had gotten really bad about "digging" in the past few months to the point where I didn't speak to Mama other than greeting her or asking about her as a teenager.

After practice while I was loading my drums in to Uncle Marc's truck Ana pulled me aside.

"What's wrong? I panicked.

"Nothing is wrong; well I don't think it is wrong . . . I mean I don't think you will think it's wrong either . . ."

"Babe . . ."

"I'm five months pregnant."

I blinked, five months, five months . . . five months would have been um end of January, I think.

"You ok?"

"Um . . . yeah, trying to think; why didn't you tell me before?"

"I wanted to be positive and I wanted to be able to tell you what we were having" She blushed. "You are unmercifully impatient."

"Well . . ."

"You're having a daughter, are you ok you're not like mad or going in to shock on me?"

"OH MY GOSH!" I yelled hugging her tight enough to cut off circulation. "Oh . . . OH" I grabbed my jacket and helmet "Take the boys make sure EVERYONES there even David!"

"Al . . . where are you . . ."

"I will be there no later than second set."

"But Al . . ."

I kissed her "I am going to have a daughter!"

"Yes, but Al . . ."

I kissed her again and took off on my Harley as fast as I legally could to make it to the baby shower store in Manchester. On the way back I called Greg, Wilson, Debbie and Madeline. Thanks to traffic backed up all the way down two for a reason I could not identify; I didn't make it back until third set and had to go right on stage.

"Five years old bright blue eyes just a little too small, just a little too different; giving his all but trying your best doesn't mean anything when you're the last out for the losing team of the local little league.

He ran he hid he cried how could he face his dad. He had let everyone down. His dad picked him up and held him close wiped his tears away. 'How could I ever not be proud of you; you are a part of me I helped to create you. I will always be here for you. Nothing you say or do will ever take away my love for you. I am here for you'

Standing tall and proud in his cap and gown on graduation day, he turned his head just in time to see his ex best friend kiss the girl he had loved. The world crashed down hard around him. He could never compare to the other kids his mom must be so ashamed.

He ran he hid he cried how could his mom love him she took his hand held it tight, whipped his tears away 'How could I ever not be proud of you; you are a part of me I helped to create you. I will always be here for you. Nothing you say or do will ever take away my love for you. I am here for you'.

What doesn't kill makes us stronger, time flies fast; as we grow older life throws curve balls in our paths. We make mistakes to make us grow. People, places, things in life we are obligated to complete and do make us who we are. We run, we hid, we cry, we pick ourselves up and try again until we get it right and hold our heads held high.

He fell in love with another man who set his world on fire beside his love he could rule the world no matter what anyone would say. They knew he had to tell his mom and dad. But once again he let them down he just couldn't compare. How could they ever love him for who he was?

He ran, he hid, he cried his man held him close and tight, wiped away his tears 'I could never not be proud of you, you hold my heart you are part of me. How could they ever not be proud of you; you are a part of them they helped to create you. They will always be here for you. Nothing you say or do will ever take away their love for you. I am here for you they're here for you.'

One day marching for his rights, for a better place for his son hand in hand with the man he loved. He heard a thought that never had occurred to him. Could it be true could he not compare where it mattered most to him.

He ran, he hid, he cried he hit his knees right there in the street and prayed he felt the lords loving embrace hold him close and tight 'How could I ever not be proud of you; you are a part of me I created you my son. I will always be here for you. Nothing you say or do will ever take away my love for you. I am here for you my son'."

"That was the last song of the night; it is called 'I am here for you' and this is last call, good night" Uncle Marc said to the audience giving me a run your Mama's mad look.

As we broke down Mom gave me a 'don't you dare question that song' look and Mama gave me a 'where have you been' look. Once the Pool hall was clear of all but whom I had asked to be there and family Mom confronted me, I think my attitude towards Mama lately was pushing her patients more than Mama's.

"I hope you have an explanation for that disappearing act" She leveled a glared at me that said I better have a good one.

"Yeah, gather every one and um . . . maybe hold Auntie Kate and Ana's dad up right."

"She's . . ."

"Shh" I smiled.

Once every one was gathered I passed out the pink bubble gum cigars "Ana is five months pregnant I am having a girl."

As predicted Ana's dad fainted but the cheers from everyone else woke Anthony "Daddy?"

"Hey pumpkin, some bubble gum?"

"No thank-you" He yawned "Why so loud?"

"You're going to have a sister."

"Awesome, tell Santa thank you" He smiled; he crawled up in to Ana's arms and went back to sleep.

Colt and Lorenzo went into a laughing fit that took My Uncles to stop.

Saturday was busy and it made Paul fussy he hated the hurry up and wait of an over scheduled day. It started at my horse show/competition, Thunderbolt and I took third place. Then while Ana took the boys to McDonald's for lunch I made sure the planetarium was set for Anthony's birthday party. He had a rocket ship ice cream cake and a UFO piñata. He didn't have a lot of friends coming but he didn't mind; he was just excited to have his first birthday party ever. I counted out and taped off the seats in the show area, the seats in the party room, and then the good bags.

At one forty five Ana brought in a very crabby, cranky, fussy Paul and an over excited spastic Anthony; Ana looked fried.

"Uh-oh, what did I miss?"

"*Your* son made me chase him up those tubes in the play place, *again*, because he didn't want to leave."

"Paul bad form" I shook my head.

"Nana says . . . Nana says . . ." Anthony bounced.

"Slow down, what did Nana say?"

"That she will meet us in the main room because Uncle Colt won't stop picking fights with Lorenzo."

"Ok, let's go greet your guest and give Paul a moment to remember that it is bad form to irritate her on a Saturday." I glanced at Paul he had spent the last three Saturdays with David and early bed because he couldn't behave.

"Ok" Anthony giggled.

"Anthony, I saw that keep your fingers out of the frosting" Ana sighed.

Anthony laughed running ahead of me down the hallway

Within fifteen minutes I had seven excited six and seven year olds running wild toward the main room for the presentation, chattering, jumping and just over all being little boys. Then they ran back to the party cake, piñata and presents.

"Thanks Daddy" Anthony hugged me when his last guest had left "It was sooo cool."

"I'm glad you had fun."

We ate dinner at the pool hall then set it up for Fallen Stars. We were opening for them tonight and before we were even letting those there just for the show in there was a line of teen and pre teen girls from the door to the road. As I promised Genevieve and Andy had a front booth with Tiny, Carter and Will; they were still the only two girls with weekend leave or just plan released. Tiffany was getting there as was Lynn but Brittany would just not listen. The offer was extended to Kevin and Kyle as well but being younger it was more up to their parents, they had also expressed extreme dislike of Fallen Stars when I told their mothers of the bands show.

"You said both nights" Genevieve accused.

"They canceled not me" I sighed already having been accused and harassed by Amelia; more power to Will she was stubborn to the core.

*　　　*　　　*

Sunday I had wanted to sleep in but there was just too much to do, two days until the wedding and I was so nervous I dropped everything I touched. The morning was spent confirming travel plans, decorations, weather, and guest seating while the boys played. That night was the rehearsal dinner; Paul and Anthony were such cute ring bearers.

Monday was just as busy the boys and I had a final tux fitting, as Anthony had shot up a good seven or eight inches and Paul at least five. After the tux fitting the boys and I fit in some much need time at the stables. After dinner they stayed with Mom and Mama while I went out with Greg, Wilson and Kenny. While Ana went out with Sam, Debbie and Madeline.

"Dude your twitching" Kenny said.

"Nerves" I blushed we were out in the woods, in the old tree house playing cards.

"I raise you three skittles" Wilson said "How can you be nervous?"

"He looks normal to me" Greg laughed.

"Geese thanks, Greg" I shook my head, "I am just afraid I will be a bad Father and or Husband."

"Not this again" Kenny groaned.

Three hands hit the back of my head.

*   *   *

I didn't sleep well and Paul new it.

"Here Daddy" Paul handed me the Orange juice.

"Thanks Monkey."

"Where's Mom?" Anthony asked.

"Umm . . . At Mr. Wittsons, I think with Sam" I yawned.

"Oh" He looked at me "Uncle Kenny is a sleep in your chair."

"I know he gave Wilson his bed and Greg has the couch."

"Oh"

The rest of the day was a lot of hurry up and wait. Finally it was two we were at the beach; I was standing in my tux next to Greg, Wilson, and Kenny. The beasts, Nick and Colt were seating guest.

"Are you well son?" The J.P. asked.

"He always looks like that" Greg laughed.

I looked at the balloons, flowers, and ribbons. I knew that at the pool hall was Ms. Gabby's lasagna. Then I looked at the boys Anthony was proudly holding the pillow with my ring, while Paul was driving his empty pillow. "SHIT!"

Kenny looked at me "Uh is something wrong?"

"Ana's ring, I left it in my work locker! Stall!" I took off running, a bunch of cameras flashed and I nearly lashed out.

Uncle Christian was parking cars. "Um, Al . . ."

"Keys to something, I left Ana's ring in my work locker, Kenny is stalling."

He looked at me and handed me the keys to his Harley "One scratch, ding, dent anything and this will be a funeral not a wedding."

"Ok" I gulped.

I drove as fast as I legally could it was hot in the tux and the breeze felt good. When I got to the center I slammed through security and into the locker room.

I looked at the ring it was still sitting in its box in the jeweler's bag.

"Aren't you supposed to be at your wedding?" Quentin looked at me from his locker.

"Epic fail" I smiled sheepishly "I forgot the ring."

"Smooth" He went back to work.

I went toward the front door then stopped and went and locked myself in the time out room. I don't know how long I was in there but I was sure Ana would hate me when I got back. Soon there was a knock on the door, Mama was standing there; I opened the door.

"I'm not ready yet my heads still spinning."

"Alexander Joseph, I am in a dress, I didn't even wear a dress for my wedding, what's wrong?"

I gave her a pointed look, the same one she had been giving me.

"Really, your over a half an hour late for your own wedding, your bride is terrified you crashed your uncle's bike . . ."

"I was afraid I would too" I blushed.

"And you want to do this now."

I just stared at the wall.

"Yep, I figured. I told Tina you were me, even if she gave birth."

"That song" I looked at her.

She gave me that pointed look; then sighed "How out of all my children are you the one that can't respect that?"

"If I don't know how you and Mom did it how will know I am doing it right? I mean look I am already screwing everything up I forgot the ring."

"So I heard" She frowned. "Ok" She sat down "Let's play the game so you will stop driving me nuts and go back to your own wedding."

"The extra J in your nick name, what's it for?"

"Really? I thought someone would have already told you that one." She laughed "It's Juliet, Juliet Jessica Marie."

"Oh, you have Grandma's name."

"No I am Jessica; I have not been Juliet since I was and infant."

"Oh um . . ."

"Why are you here, goof ball, it's your wedding?" She laughed hugging me.

"I know, and I know she is going to hate me, but I guess I panicked."

"She doesn't hate you."

"Did you panic at your wedding?"

"Nope, I was sure, C.J. panicked for me" She laughed. "Why the Panic?"

"I'm nervous, the camera flashes and what if she says no?"

"Alex, strongly doubt she will say no, you know your father had that sensitivity to camera flashes too."

"Yeah, mom told me. Why do you hate Grandma so much? I mean your Mom."

"She is not my mom, Alex," There was venom in her voice "She is my mother, she gave birth to me, but she didn't raise me. Your uncle Marc and Kork raised me." She looked like she was going to cry, spit fire and deck me all at once. She took a deep breath "So maybe, somehow, you have my temper, and so you know I don't hate her. I don't know her well and we have strong differing opinions. I agreed to visit her for certain thing the day you were born."

"Oh" I nodded "So, it's like pushing to polar opposite magnets together?"

"Yep."

"But I am twenty-two . . ."

"I know and she is still trying to tell me how to raise you."

I laughed.

"Talk to me what's scaring you most?"

"Failing. Why do you ride your horse so odd?"

She laughed "You can't figure that one out yourself? I know you have more questions than that."

"Well I know the hurdles but . . ."

"Speed" She laughed "And because like I have told your Uncle a hundred times horses need hugs too."

"Oh" I laughed. "A.J. said you didn't talk much."

"Couldn't talk."

"Why?"

"Don't know, I talk fine now."

"Um ok" I laughed "No one found out why?"

"My daddy was busy and Marc was five. He shrugged and said maybe she is like Troy and will talk when she has actually has something to say."

"Did you have something to say?"

"Yep, had plenty to say, I just couldn't get the thoughts to come out of my mouth no matter how hard I tried. When C.J. and I started school Henry and Kyle decided I was mute and taught me sign language."

I laughed.

"Why do you think you will fail?"

I sighed "I forgot the ring and every time I look at her my brain freezes."

Mama laughed "Really, that's why. Alex, I put the ring on your mother's middle finger and twenty five years later the sight of my beautiful girl still causes my brain to freeze. Welcome to love."

"What if I upset her again?"

"It happens, people fight, your mother and I still fight."

"You make it look so easy."

"Well it is far from easy, we have had time to practice it. Ana knows you and loves you just the way you are. She doesn't want or need perfection just you to be you. The same with my grandsons they don't need superman, just you; they love you just the way you are. Little kids, Al, they know bad, when they see it and that's not you."

"What were you like at my age?"

"At twenty two I was balancing a music Career with a one year old. Tina and I were fighting, and still grieving the loss of your father he was a very good friend and we had loved him dearly. We had moved in with your grandparents and Uncle in Italy. I was going back and forth between Italy and here. I barely slept and I was unpleasant."

"So that's why we were in Italy?"

"No, Italy was my choice" She laughed "I like Italy and it was easier to tour Europe living in Europe. It was a balance to try and work out the fighting with Tina. On top of that I was fighting a few demons of my own. Your mother had a regular job and was trying to publish her first book. Many night's I ended up taking you on stage with me. And sweetie I was never a wake and never sure of myself back then, and you, your diaper was always backwards, your shoes always on the wrong feet, and I think when I had you I remembered a bib once maybe twice."

I laughed.

I made your Uncles cringe but not one of them stopped me. You're Aunt Kate and your Uncle Christian held their breath a lot. I am almost positive that your Grandma J nearly had a heart attack a few time and a migraine a lot I never gave you a pacifier I told you that's nice scream all you want."

I laughed "What were you like as a teenager? Uncle Christian and Uncle Chris said you are why work boots aren't allowed in the school."

"Hmm I knew that one would come back to bite me in the back side" She laughed "I was horrific, just a plan flat out brat."

"Like that song?"

"Worse, minus the cops, I cut as you know and I had the attitude that went with it. I had no desire to stop cutting for anyone or anything. I was mean, closer to the edge of cruel, to everyone and everything. And oh did I put your father through his paces." She smiled "Sadly he will not get to see the profound change you and your brothers have made in my life and your mothers. Your mother and I fought and fought; I'd pick fights just because I could and she knew it and she'd just walk away and let me fight with myself. I had a huge chip on my shoulder and I didn't let anyone close to me the closest was your Mom or your Uncle Christian. I felt I had every right to rage war with the world, my father had died on my birthday and I was teased more like tortured at school, so I let my temper control me. It was not my finest hour."

"Like me in high school?"

"Worse, you would pick fights with people actually upsetting you; I would just deck the first person that came within ten feet of me because I could. I nearly got expelled so many times I thought your uncle was going to strangle me. And oh was I mouthy and the swearing" She shook her head "Every other word out of my mouth was a cuss word, even in church. Yeah that's the face Marc made; it is a miracle Marc didn't kill me. I locked myself in my room or the school art room a lot."

"Uncle Marc didn't get you help?"

"He tried, I spent a lot of time grounded, working, extra chores and that floor scrubbing those boys are so terrified of I owned it every other week I was scrubbing some floor with a tooth brush. I had counseling but with work and school and this and that I didn't make time for it and Marc couldn't enforce it. The day after you were born is the day I made the effort and started to pull myself together. And the schools boot rule yeah that was me."

I cringed.

"Hey, hey don't you make that face at me there is good reason, you asked now listen the class bull tried, and trust me it was tried he bit off more than he could chew. But he tried to 'teach me' how to like guys after trying to kidnap me. I kicked him hard enough to cause permanent damage."

"Ooo Mama" I cringed and crossed my legs I couldn't even began to fathom the pain she had caused that man.

"He never tried that again, in fact he has stayed very clear of my path ever since. But Alexander, that mean person I am not her any more, I will never be her again I learned to love myself for me so I could love others."

"*I know*" I cringed again at the thought of a well placed boot there . . .

"You know, you know you're late to your own wedding, smart ass?"

"Yeah" I laughed "We better get going before Uncle Christian sends a search party for you." I shifted "I hate ties."

"Me too"

I raised an eye brow "You don't wear ties?"

"Nope, just constantly having to tie C.J.'s" She laughed "Are you satisfied?"

"Why didn't you want us to know?"

"I wanted . . . I wanted you to never know the person I was she is in the past and I am not her. I didn't want you boys to think poorly of me,

I didn't want to think about it myself, honestly. Most of all, though, I wanted you boys to grow up and form who you were on your own without thinking you had to do something just because your mother or I did it."

"Oh" I nodded "I don't think we could ever think poorly of you; we love you."

"Thank-you, I love you boys too."

"Oh and Mama one more thing?"

"What?"

"A.J. and I have a bet going; the calendar charts . . . you or Uncle Christian?"

She laughed so hard I thought she was going to stop breathing. "Neither," She laughed harder shaking her head, "They are for C.J., his memory is that Awful. I mean they are great organization and all but they are all for him. They were Marc's solution to C.J.'s memory problems. It just stuck some things stick, like nick names. C.J.'s full name is Christopher James Jacob Williams. Oh and speaking of Names I would prefer if you didn't tell your beastly twin brothers my given name; well at least until they are grown men with boys of their own."

I laughed "No worries."

We took Uncle Christian's bike back to the beach I never knew that Mama knew how to ride on the back of a motorcycle but then it occurred to me that my father had two bikes, and Uncle Chris and Uncle Christian each had one. Mama told everyone that it was bad traffic and winked at me. I took a deep breath still panicking and took my place next to the J.P. and Kenny. Everything was really surreal as the music started I watched the boys now with both rings, then the brides maids and the maid of honor walked down the aisle; or well in between the chairs, flowers and ribbons on the beach. I gulped as I saw Ana in her mother's wedding gown, her hair was French braided with flowers in it.

And that's when it happened it was like a cosmic click when Ana's dad placed her hand in mine and the J.P said "Today we are gathered here . . ." I looked into her eyes and I got it, I knew everything was going to be ok. Perfect no but life wasn't meant to be perfect. I would always be Just Alex to her and that is what she wanted, because I didn't need to be anyone other than just me. I would have bad days, no sleep, night mares and as long as I had Ana and my children all three or more if we had more it would be ok. I would walk into a Buddy or Curtis fight at work and come out looking like I lost a boxing match, have to separate bickering girls, watch the kids at work struggle with all the levels of the program and only half of them ever fully making it, brave large crowds at the mall or Wal-Mart. My family would drive me nuts, I wouldn't always have an answer, some days would be long tiring and occasionally painful, but I could handle it because at the end of the day waiting for me was a wife and kids who loved me for just being, Alex. And as long as I did my best; me is all I would ever have to be. Just Alexander Joseph Williams.

AUTHOR'S NOTE

There are a lot of strong, 'deep' topics in this book. Addictions of any kind are dangerous weather it is self mutilation, drugs, smoking or alcohol there is help out there for it. Like 'Alex' I no longer cut. I won't tell you don't cut but I will tell you I wish better for you; as I am a strong believer in not being a hypocrite. As for the others I will say please don't you are worth more than that.

Eating disorders are serious things, too, and there is also help for that. Skipping meals can cause issues with your blood sugar, just as over eating can too. Purging can rip the lining of you esophagus from the constant stomach acid being forced aggressively up it.

Child abuse is ALWAYS the wrong way to go if you feel that you are going to hurt your child there are programs to teach you how to properly discipline a child and control your temper. If you know someone is being abused, the right thing to do is call your local child protective service or local police department, no matter what. If you are still not sure where to turn for help 211 is nationwide and will know. It' also offers help for suicide and other problems.